Adbhut

Also by Meena Arora Nayak

The Kathasaritsagara of Somadeva: A Retelling
The Blue Lotus: Myths and Folktales of India
A Dust Storm in Delhi
Evil in the Mahabharata
Endless Rain
About Daddy
In the Aftermath
The Puffin Book of Legendary Lives

Adbhut

MARVELLOUS CREATURES
of INDIAN MYTH *and* FOLKLORE

MEENA ARORA NAYAK

Illustrated by Krishna Bala Shenoi

ALEPH

ALEPH

ALEPH BOOK COMPANY
An independent publishing firm
promoted by *Rupa Publications India*

First published in India in 2022
by Aleph Book Company
7/16 Ansari Road, Daryaganj
New Delhi 110 002

Copyright © Meena Arora Nayak 2022

The author has asserted her moral rights.

All rights reserved.

No part of this publication may be reproduced,
transmitted, or stored in a retrieval system, in any form
or by any means, without permission in writing from
Aleph Book Company.

ISBN: 978-93-91047-23-8

3 5 7 9 10 8 6 4 2

Printed in India

This book is sold subject to the condition that it shall
not, by way of trade or otherwise, be lent, resold, hired
out, or otherwise circulated without the publisher's
prior consent in any form of binding or cover other
than that in which it is published.

For Rihan, our little marvel

Tyger Tyger, burning bright,
In the forests of the night;
What immortal hand or eye,
Dare frame thy fearful symmetry?

—*The Tyger*, William Blake

CONTENTS

Author's Note   xiii

Introduction   xix

Creatures of the Sky
1. Simurgh the Soul's Reality   3
2. Ziz the Bird of Chaos   6
3. Kaka Bhusundi the Time-travelling Crow   7
4. Byangoma and Byangomi   12
5. Hiraman the Talking Parrot   14
6. Jatayu the Braveheart   19
7. Peacock the Beautiful, the Sad   22
8. Chitta Baaz   25
9. The Chakor and His Love and Longing   27
10. Garuda the Devourer   28
11. Phoenix—Reborn from Its Own Ashes   35

Creatures of the Sea
12. Matsya the Cosmic Fish   39
13. Leviathan the Sea Monster   44
14. Makara the Immortal Crocodile   46
15. Kurma the World Tortoise   49
16. Timingila that Once Was   51
17. Varaha the Good and Evil Boar   53
18. The Golden Hamsa   57

19. Badava the Submarine Mare   60

Creatures of the Earth
20. Behemoth the Land Monster   65
21. The She-Camel   67
22. Akoman the Evil Mind   70
23. The Golden Mongoose   72
24. The Dog that Guards the Judgement Bridge   76
25. Reem a Mountain with Horns   78
26. Tekhumiavi a Dreamscape   80
27. Jambavana the Monkey Bear   82
28. Uchchaihshravas the Cosmic Horse   86
29. Kuyutha the Cosmic Bull   88
30. Nandi the Dharma Bull   90
31. Buddha the White Elephant   93
32. Mahisa the Majestic   96
33. Airavata the King of Elephants   99
34. The Holy Cow: Prithvi, Surabhi, Dharma   102

Other Creatures of Air, Water, and Land
Worms, Insects, Reptiles, and Dragons
35. Azhi Dahaka the Corrupter of the Order   109
36. The Serpent in the Garden of Eden   112
37. Shesha Naag the Endless One   115
38. Takshaka an Ophidian Epitome   118
39. Pakhangpa the Guardian Python   122
40. Mandeha the Sandhill   125
41. Bhramari the Beehive Goddess   127
42. Shamir the Stone-cutting Worm   129

43. The Caterpillar Man	131
44. Ants—Teachers of Humility	132

Creations of Amalgam

45. Buraq the Shining One	136
46. Nariphon the Plant Women	140
47. Adne Sadeh the Human Plants	142
48. Dadhikravana the Bird–Horse and Hayagriva the Horse-headed	143
49. Yali a Synthesis in Stone	146
50. Chalkydri the Angels of the Sun	148
51. Kinnara—Perhaps a Man	149
52. Sharabha a Shiva Avatar	151
53. Gandabherunda a Vishnu Avatar	155
54. Navagunjara a Unity	157
55. Harappan Chimera	160
Acknowledgments	163
Sources	165

AUTHOR'S NOTE

I started this book with a list of creatures that are truly fantastical in physical form: Navagunjara, the nine-animal chimera of the Sarala Mahabharata; Behemoth and Leviathan, the immense beasts of chaos from the Bible; Sharabha and Gandabherunda, the composite beast avatars of Shiva and Vishnu; and others like these. Then the pandemic hit, and within a few weeks of lockdown, strange phenomena began to occur in cities and towns across the world. Dolphins were sighted in the Bosporus in Istanbul. In the canals of Venice, people began to see shimmering fish, instead of the murkiness and smoke of water taxis.[1] In San Francisco, people began to hear trilling birdsongs, not having to contend with the noise of cars.[2] In Gurgaon, one morning, birdwatchers caught sight of the never before seen desert finch, a bird who inhabits the high altitudes of Balochistan.[3] And, for the first time in sixty years, four majestic whooper swans suddenly appeared in Kashmir. Sadly, two of them were shot down by poachers.[4]

In my own garden, I started noticing more red cardinals,

---

[1] Julia Jacobo, 'Venice canals are clear enough to see fish as coronavirus halts tourism in the city', *ABC News*, 18 March 2020.
[2] Ruth Williams, 'Pandemic Shutdown Altered Bay Area Birdsongs', *The Scientist*, 24 September 2020.
[3] Prayag Arora-Desai, 'Desert finch sighted for the first time in India', *Hindustan Times*, 22 November 2020.
[4] Firdous Hassan, 'Four rare whooper swans spotted in Kashmir, poachers kill two of them', *Kashmir Monitor*, 23 November 2020.

blue jays, and woodpeckers. Once I even caught sight of a hummingbird hovering over the gladiolas. Then, one morning, I discovered a family of deer, eating the green peppers in my vegetable patch. I thought about getting my camera, but when I saw the mother eyeing the white moon flowers on the vine I had painstaking grown after many failed attempts, I ran out to shoo her away. And, just for a moment, she and I stood eye to eye. She, with her dark, luminous, blank gaze, and me, stunned at the marvel of it all. At that moment, I realized what was lacking in my vision of the book: the sense of wonder that comes from perceiving something marvellous, which is necessarily a viewer's response. Hence, even a simple cardinal or deer is marvellous; we have just forgotten how to see the marvel. The Qur'an says that each being in creation is an ayah, a miracle—a sign from Allah.

After this realization, I widened my scope of research, and my list began to include creatures that appear to be ordinary but are extraordinary in their significance because of their sociocultural affiliations. Hence, the book I was going to subtitle 'Fantastical Creatures' became a book of 'Marvellous Creatures'.

I have selected fifty-five marvellous creatures from the myths and folklore of India's various cultures. These are divided into five sections: Creatures of the Sky; Creatures of the Sea; Creatures of Earth; Other Creatures of Air, Water, and Land; and Creations of Amalgam. The first three are cosmographic realms established in most creation myths; the creatures of the fourth section exist between these realms, the last section includes chimeric creatures that exist only in the imagination.

All the tales about these creatures in this book are

treated differently; no two pieces are alike. The only common modality is a description of their physical form to allow the reader to visualize them. Some stories are straight up myths, because the myth itself is fascinating; in some I have included an analysis, because the creature is more fascinating in the way it has been perceived in social, cultural, and religious milieus; for instance, the story of the serpent in the Garden of Eden. Other stories, like that of the parrot or the simurgh, examine literary and cultural references. Some creatures are storied for their symbolic meaning, such as Guru Gobind Singh's Chitta Baaz, and still others, like the chakor, for their poetic metaphor. Some of the creatures belong to many cultures across the world, such as the phoenix or the bull, while others, like the Quranic she-camel, are significant in a specific tradition. In a couple of stories, like that of Vishnu's fish avatar, Matsya, I have included three different versions of the same myth from three different sources to show how the creature evolved in literary traditions. Conversely, a few creatures have two or more separate stories in the same narrative to demonstrate their polygonal significance.

Readers will surely question why some well-known creatures, like Narasimha, the man-lion avatar of Vishnu, are not included. This is because I have already told their story in an earlier book. On the other hand, some stories have to be repeated; they are so interconnected with other tales that they must be told as necessary contexts. Hence, readers will get snippets of the snakes' birth myth in several pieces. I also want to beg the reader's indulgence for those stories in which the contextual myth is minimalized. Since these are short whimsical tales, I did not want to weigh them down with too much of a back story. These 'missing' backgrounds are mostly common myths with which readers may already be familiar. And, if they are not, I hope the reference will trigger their interest and encourage them to read the myths elsewhere.

The tales are arranged to provide a spectrum—from sacred to profane, from creation to destruction, from myth to metaphor. Some stories are arranged to create a relationship; for instance, the story of Shesha Naag is followed by the tale of Takshaka, because they are siblings. Similarly, Kuyutha, the cosmic bull from Islam, and Nandi, the Hindu dharma bull, are in sequence, because they are both sustainers of cosmic order. The last two pieces in the book, Navagunjara and the Harappan Chimera, also appear to have a parallel relationship. However, the former, a nine-animal composite from Sarala Das's Odia Mahabharata, is from the fifteenth century CE, and the latter, a seven-animal composite engraved on the Indus Valley seals, is dated to about 2800 BCE. They are both unique creatures of imagination, created millennia apart; yet there is an uncanny similarity between them. The reason I have put them together at the end of the book is because their resemblance evokes questions: did the pre-Vedic chimera continue to exist in cosmic memory till the fifteenth century? Did Sarala Das know the significance of this amalgamation? He was a simple farmer, and the Indus Valley script is undeciphered. Also, as far as I know, there is no evidence to explain either the seal or Navagunjara. Perhaps, I am simply caught in awe of these creatures and am seeing a connection where there is none; maybe, their affinity is only coincidental, or, perhaps, it isn't. I leave it to the reader to draw their own conclusions.

I want to end this note with the title of the book—*Adbhut*.

Adbhut is a rasa in the *Natyashastra*. It is the viewer's response to the sentiment of the marvellous. Its enduring state is vismaya, or astonishment, and its transitory states, (when people encounter the marvellous), are paralysis, perspiration, horripilation, impulsivity, confusion, giddiness, excitement, frenzy, immobility, and loss of consciousness. When the rasa of adbhut is enacted on stage, it is depicted with 'widening of the eyes, fixing the gaze, exclaiming "Ha, Ha, Ha", applauding, shedding tears (of joy), trembling, perspiring, fluttering the end of a dhoti or sari or quivering the face and fingers.'[5]

This book is a narrative enactment of adbhut creatures. Dear reader, be astonished!

---

[5]*Nāṭyaśāstra of Bharata Muni*, Part 1, Ch. 6, tr. Manomohan Ghosh, Calcutta: Asiatic Society of Bengal, 1951.

INTRODUCTION

Mysterium tremendum et fascinans! Mysterious, terrible, and terrifying, yet fascinating and irresistible! This is how the twentieth century theologian, Rudolf Otto, characterizes the holy. Fantastical creatures, too, can be described similarly. They are magical and marvellous, oftentimes, beautiful, and, sometimes, monstrous; but, even in their monstrousness, they are fascinating and compelling.

The image that comes to mind when one thinks of a fantastical creature is of a chimeric amalgam fashioned in the imaginative mind of mythmakers and folklorists, or of a preternatural being whose physical form is almost impossible to imagine. However, the quality of fantasticality cannot be based only in the single dimension of the physical plane; these creatures are also fantastic because of what they signify. Metaphors, paradigms, histories, beliefs, and cultural ethos are all encapsulated in their being. Hence, even commonplace, everyday animals of the real world become marvellous when invested with this affluence.

In medieval Europe, naturalists and mystics, captivated by the natural history of animals, sought a divine connection through them. Consequently, there was a trend of compiling compendiums of fantastic creatures. Following the example of the encyclopedic *Naturalis Historia* of Pliny the Elder and the Greek didactic text, *Physiologus*, these texts started a genre of bestiary that elucidated Christian morality through anecdotal fables about beasts and birds. These beings were not only depicted with extravagant details, they were also given allegorical meanings. For example, the unicorn was perceived as the purity of Christ, the Phoenix as Jesus's resurrection, and the fire-breathing dragon represented the Devil. The animals included in these texts were both exotic, such as lions and tigers, and imaginary, such as unicorns, griffins, and dragons. Also, many manuscripts, like the *Aberdeen Bestiary*, were lavishly illuminated.

By the end of the medieval period, Christian bestiaries were no longer trending. The convention, however, continues till today in different genres: moralistic tales for children, literary writings in the style of Jorge Luis Borges's *The Book of Imaginary Beings*, and monster compendiums for role-playing games (RPGs) of popular culture.

In India, the tradition of animal lore is, at least, as old as *Panchatantra*, whose oldest extant version is dated to about 200 BCE. However, there is no specific heritage of anthologizing fantastical creatures, as in the bestiaries. Perhaps, this is because in the myth and folklore of India, birds and animals have always been more than just allegories or symbols of religiosity. They are part of cosmogonies and cosmographies and are integral to the very flux of cultural norms. They delineate relationships of the human and divine; they encase archetypes and actuate behaviours; their references are part of the idiom, and their metaphors not only bridge myth and folklore but also communities. They can be therianthropic (part beast, part human) or wholly zoomorphic (animal). They can be vehicles of gods, or gods themselves. They are signifiers of the transmigration of the soul, or the eternal soul itself; they can define human characteristics or be astrological emblems of planets, shaping human idiosyncrasies. They can be religious, as in myth, or secular, as in folklore. But no matter what form they take, they are intrinsically woven into India's cultures of oral, artistic, and written histories.

THERIOMORPHIC FORMS

In myth, marvellous creatures are often deities in theriomorphic form (animal form with a combination of human and animal characteristics). Scholars believe that therianthropism or theriomorphy may be an approximation of ancient tribal systems of iconography, such as totemism, in which a group of people identified with a plant, animal, or bird. It may also be a vestige of early zoolatry and animal cults. For example, the makara or crocodile in pre-Vedic water cosmology may have been a cult animal in the Indus Valley, worshipped because of its 'mysterious and fearful presence in the seas.'[1] The makara was also connected to fertility; hence, it was considered a soma animal, an animal associated with the elixir of immortality that was drilled from the bottom of the ocean. Thus, in later iconography, it came to be depicted as the vahana of Ganga, who facilitates the transmigration of the indestructible soul. Similarly, Shiva's vahana, Nandi the bull, may have been an iteration of the cult of the divine bull that existed in many ancient societies; for example, the Apis Bull of Memphis (city in ancient Egypt), the Minoan bull of Crete, and the Bull of Heaven in Mesopotamia.

One of the most prevalent cults, which still has

---

[1] Steven Darian, 'The Other Face of the Makara', *Artibus Asiae*, 1976, Vol. 38, No. 1, 1976, pp. 29–36.

practitioners in India, is of the serpent. From the earliest times, snakes have been associated with fertility and the mother goddess creatrix. The snake, in its varied forms of dragon and python and in its ambiguous duality of good and evil, is a ubiquitous symbol in almost all world mythologies. Indian mythological traditions too, especially Hindu and Buddhist, abound with this creature, and in tribal cultures, such as the Meitei and Chothe of Manipur, people worship it as the python guardian god, Pakhangpa. Even in Indian folklore, the serpent, especially the cobra, is a recurrent character. The common belief about it is that after it has lived a hundred years, it acquires a nagamani (jewel) on its hood and the ability to take any shape, even that of a human. These abilities make it an ideal candidate for deification.

Animal apotheoses may have given way to composite deities, such as Ganesha and Hanuman. However, even in hybridity, the animals retain their entity, which gives the deities the combined cognizance of a human and animal. Also, in purely anthropomorphic representations, the gods' zoomorphic connections are still clearly evident. A good example of the gradual transformation from animal to human-like, and the coexistence of both forms, is in Vishnu's avatars. His first three avatars are non-human—Matsya the fish; Kurma the tortoise; and Varaha the boar. This is followed by the man-lion hybrid, Narasimha, and his fifth avatar, the Vamana, is the human-like dwarf who increases in size with Vishnu's divine maya. Subsequent to that, all of Vishnu's avatars are fully anthropomorphic. Worthy of note is that the divinity of Vishnu preserves the attributes of all the animal forms he assumes; for instance, his first three avatars associate him with the ocean; hence, one of his enduring images is of him sleeping on the coils of the thousand-hooded cobra Shesha-Ananta, in the middle of the primordial ocean. Similarly, since he becomes Kurma (tortoise) to serve as the base for the churning stick in the Samudra Manthan creation myth, he is invoked during Vastu puja when the replica of a tortoise is placed in the foundation of the building. This Kurmashila bestows on the structure the longevity and stability of the tortoise's shell.[2]

ZOOMORPHIC VAHANAS

In Hindu myth, most deities are depicted with an emblematic animal mount, a vahana. 'The etymology of the word "vahana" is derived from the Sanskrit verbal root "vah", which means "to carry", "to draw a cart", "to guide horses", etc. During festival processions, these iconic vahanas are used to transport the idol from the sanctity of the temple to the outside world. Thus, vahanas fulfill the task of connecting the human and divine realms.'[3] A vahana also completes the divine aggregate; that is why it is included in the iconography of the god or goddess. For instance, Durga's lion represents kingship; hence when she wins victory over the asuras, her supremacy echoes that of the lion over all other beasts. For this reason, one of Durga's names is Simhavahini—one who rides the lion. In some cases, the vahana is representative of the god's tempering of the animal's potency; therefore, when Shiva rides the bull,

---

[2] Devangana Desai, 'Kūrma Imagery in Indian Art and Culture', *Artibus Asiae*, 2009, Vol. 69, No. 2, 2009, pp. 317–33.
[3] Aleksandra Wenta, 'The Great Ārdrā Darśanam Festival: Performing Śaiva Ritual Texts in Contemporary Chidambaram', *International Journal of Hindu Studies*, Vol. 17, No. 3, December 2013, pp. 371–98.

who represents virility, he is demonstrating his control over sexual desire. Some vahanas are also a means of assimilation, enabling a deity to incorporate a cult into his/her corpus. For instance, by Ganga riding the makara, who was a fertility god associated with soma in water cosmology, the Makara cult was assimilated in the river goddess mythos.

Emblematizing animal vahanas is also a part of Jyotisha, the Hindu astrological system, and, just as the vahana's characteristics fuse with the god, so do they reflect in the influence of nakshatras or lunar mansions. The twenty-seven nakshatras in Jyotisha each correspond to an animal; consequently, a person born in a particular asterism demonstrates traits associated with that animal. For example, the vahana of the Ashwini nakshatra is the horse, which is identified with Ashwin Kumars, the beautiful, horse-headed twins. Therefore, a person born under the influence of this asterism is forward looking, resolute, hardworking, and physically attractive. These animal attributes become especially significant for a marriage alliance when horoscopes are matched to see if the personalities of the couple are compatible.

SYMBOLS OF CHAOS AND CONFLICT
Aside from representing order-sustaining deiform, animals can also be symbols of chaos. For instance, monstrous beings, like Behemoth and Leviathan in the Book of Job in the Bible, are related to the abyss and threaten God's order. God has to keep them in check to prevent them from destroying creation. Often, these were also apologues of political upheavals. For instance, scholars believe that the beings of Biblical traditions were 'allegorical referents'

of 'the powerful states of ancient Egypt and Assyria' that threatened the Kingdom of Israel.[4] Similarly, Azhi Dahaka, the cosmic dragon of Zoroastrianism, was an allegory of the Arab suppression of Persia, which led to the fall of the Sassanid empire and the diminution of Zoroastrianism.

Some of the most fascinating creatures in Hindu myth and folklore were also conceived in conflict. Religio-political disputations and skirmishes between different sects and belief systems led to the creation of astounding composites that were clearly a bid by adherents for one-upmanship. Case in point: after the Vaishnavas gave Vishnu his ferocious man-lion avatar of Narasimha to destroy the daitya king, Hiranyakashipu, Shaivites, fearing Vishnu's ascendency, created the terrible Sharabha, an eight-legged bird-lion to pacify Narasimha. And, to counter Sharabha, the Vaishnavas then created Gandabherunda, an eight-headed bird with talons and a beak so sharp that he shredded Sharabha to pieces. Not to be left out from this battle for domination, the devotees of Shaktism also created their own composite— Pratyangira, the goddess with a human body and lion's face; although, in the manner of the feminine divine, she serves more as a balancing force than a contender.

Formidable beasts representing darkness or evilness may be an expression of theodicy in theistic systems. They vindicate God from the moral evil that exists by allowing Him to overpower the forces of evil.[5] In non-theistic traditions, such as those of Hinduism, there is no such Problem of Evil. However, in India, the transformation of a village god into

---

[4]Patricia Springborg, 'Hobbes's Biblical Beasts: Leviathan and Behemoth', *Political Theory*, Vol. 23, No. 2, May 1995, pp. 353–75.
[5]Ibid.

an adversary of a pan-Indian deity creates a structure of a somewhat similar subjugation: the village god is mythicized as a monstrous being and then defeated by the 'greater' god/goddess to be assimilated in the larger myth. A good example is Mahisa, the buffalo asura that Durga slays in the *Devi Mahatmya*. In many village myths (still prevalent in Tamil Nadu), Mahisa is the much-ritualized Buffalo King, Potu Raja, who, in some rituals is even married to the goddess.[6] However, in the larger Shakta traditions, he is the Goddess's foe and is killed by her. During the battle, he shapeshifts from buffalo to elephant to lion to human, and in the latter form, he regains a transformed ipseity through Durga's benevolence. In Assam, Odisha, and Bengal, the buffalo is sacrificed in honour of Goddess Durga, 'the ritual claiming that the buffalo symbolizes evil and darkness hence the worshipper is purged of his dross vicariously by partaking in the sin-and-expiation rite.'[7]

HUMAN RELATIONSHIP

Another element of the fabulous in certain animals and birds is their intimate relationship with humans. Humans and animals have a uterine connection from the beginning of time. In most belief systems, all living things—plants, animals, birds, humans—were created at the same time, by either the same impulse of a monotheistic supreme divine or through the dismemberment of a primordial being. The

---

[6]David Shulman, 'The Murderous Bride: Tamil Versions of the Myth of Devī and the Buffalo-Demon', *History of Religions*, Vol. 16, No. 2, November 1976, pp. 120–46.
[7]Sukumari Bhattacharji, *The Indian Theogony*, New Delhi: Penguin Books, India, 2000, p. 168.

'Purusha-Sukta' of the Rig Veda states:

> When the gods spread the sacrifice with Man (Purusha), as the offering.... They anointed the Man, the sacrifice born at the beginning, upon the sacred grass. With him the gods, Sadhyas, and sages sacrificed. From the sacrifice in which everything was offered, the melted fat was collected, and he (Creator or Purusha) made it into those beasts who live in the air, in the forest, and in villages.... Horses were born from it, and those other animals that have two rows of teeth; cows were born from it, and from it goats and sheep were born.[8]

From the Genesis story in the Bible:

> On the fourth day, God said, 'Let the waters teem with countless creatures, and let birds fly above the earth across the vault of heaven.' God then created the sea-monsters and all living creatures that move and swarm in the waters, according to their kind, and every kind of bird.... On the fifth day, God said, 'Let the earth bring forth living creatures, according to their kind: cattle, reptiles, and wild animals, all according to their kind.... Then God said 'Let us make man in our image....' So God created man in his own image.[9]

The Qur'an says, 'There is not an animal (that lives) on earth, nor a being that flies on its wings, but (forms part of) communities like you. Nothing have We omitted from the

---

[8] *The Hymns of the Ṛigveda*, tr. Ralph T. H. Griffith, Benares: E. J. Lazarus and Co, 1890.
[9] Genesis 20–26, *The New English Bible*, Oxford: Oxford University Press, 1970.

Book, and they (all) shall be gathered to their Lord at the end' (6:38).[10]

In tribal cultures, this connection between man and human is even more pronounced. In fact, sometimes, the inception of the universe itself is with animals or bird ancestors. For example, in Santhal belief, the Creator first created the goose and gander, Has and Hasil, and from their eggs, human beings were formed.[11] In a similar vein, most Naga tribes believe that the first tiger and the first man were brothers—sons of the same mother, who separated only because of their differing instincts and behaviours. Hence, a man's soul can easily transfer into a tiger's body. That is why for the Nagas, it is taboo for men to kill tigers, for it would be tantamount to fratricide.

The idea of the transmigration of the soul is, perhaps, an echo of this continuum. It is a common notion among Hindus, Buddhists, and Sikhs that the world consists of 84 million species, which include all animal and human forms, and a soul suffers through all of these before reaching liberation. For this reason, most religious systems in India attribute moral agency to birds and animals—the cognizance to incur karma. This is most evident in the animal symbolism of Jain tirthankaras. Seventeen of the twenty-four tirthankaras are associated with animals and birds—some of them through their earlier incarnations; for instance, Mahavira is represented by a lion, because he was a lion in his previous birth, and Rishabhdeva's symbol is the bull,

---

[10] *The Holy Qur'ān*, tr. Abdullah Yusuf Ali, Lahore: Shaik Muhammad Ashraf Publishers, 1937.
[11] Meena Arora Nayak, 'Pilcu Haran and Pilcu Budhi', *Blue Lotus: Myths and Folktales of India*, New Delhi: Aleph Book Company, 2018, pp. 11–13.

because he is affiliated with farming through a past life. The Buddha, too, experienced many animal births, which are described in the Jatakas, the Buddha's birth stories. In each of these births, he is conscious of his karmic, intellectual, and moral growth.

Man's relationship with birds is more of a mystical kind. Most often, birds represent the Self and the soul's journey. Their wings are considered magical, because their flight represents transcendence; therefore, when birds soar, they seem to be touching heaven itself. An excellent portrayal of this symbolism is in Farid ud-Din Attar's *The Conference of the Birds,* where a group of thirty birds seek communion with the divine, who is allegorized as the Simurgh. He appears before them like a mirror in which they see themselves and, when they realize that they are seeing the soul's reality, they attain fana—liberation through annihilation. The Hamsa is another bird of mystical symbolism. The Hamsa Upanishad says Hamsa is life breath; the Brihadaranyaka Upanishad says it is the eternal soul. Sarasvati, the goddess of learning, rides the Hamsa, and in Gandhara art, the Buddha's fingers and toes are webbed like a hamsa bird to show the control his intellect has over his actions and desire.[12] Similarly, Buraq, the bird-horse composite, is a Sufi 'symbol of the "human breath" by means of which the mystic travels to the world of the spirit and contemplation of the Divine'...an otherworldly 'carriage to cover the intellectual distance of understanding Allah's reality.'[13]

---

[12]Stella Kramrisch, 'Image of Buddha from Gandhara', *Philadelphia Museum of Art Bulletin*, Spring, Vol. 61, No. 289, 1966, pp. 36–39.

[13]Ron Buckley, 'The "Burāq": Views from the East and West', *Arabica*, 2013, T. 60, Fasc. 5, 2013, pp. 569–601.

In the theistic systems of Judaism, Christianity, and Islam, animals are not equivalent to, or representative of the human experience. God gives man 'rule over the fish in the sea, the birds of heaven, and every living thing that moves upon the earth' (Genesis 28). However, they are sometimes symbolic of the divine; for example, the Phoenix represents Christ's Resurrection. Moreover, all creatures have the ability to communicate with the divine. For instance, the Qur'an tells the story of a she-camel who is slaughtered by the Thamud tribe. When Allah hears the cries of her calf, He punishes the perpetrators. In a similar manner, creatures can also glorify God; for instance, the Chalkydri and the Phoenix in Christian and Jewish traditions herald the sun every morning and, at the command of God, shade it with their wings so as to protect the people on earth from its fiery rays.

In folklore, which synthesizes the real and imaginative without the adhesive of religious mysticism, man and animal are blended into a world that appears wholly believable. Folklore fulfils a purpose—to teach life lessons. Hence, when in an Ao Naga folktale (included in the book), a caterpillar becomes a man to entice two young women, the simple caterpillar on a tree branch becomes a mysterious creature with dark designs. In Bengali folklore, the birds Byangoma and Byangomi (also included in the book) communicate with people in human voices and heal them with a salve made from their droppings, thus, teaching people the worth of harmonizing with nature. In fact, talking birds are a common motif in folklore, especially the Indian parrot, who can mimic a human voice. This talent of speech, along with their mystical connotations, makes birds ideal mediators between the human and animal world.

This animal–human reciprocity is not just an Indian belief; many cultures across the world have similar ideologies. For example, the Eskimologist, Knud Rasmussen, cites this belief of the Inuit people of the Arctic regions: 'In the very earliest time, when both people and animals lived on earth, a person could become an animal if he wanted to, and an animal could become a human being. Sometimes they were people and sometimes animals and there was no difference.'[14]

---

[14]Knud Rasmussen qtd. in Kimberly Patton, 'Caught with Ourselves in the Net of Life and Time', *A Communion of Subjects: Animals in Religion, Science & Ethics*, Paul Waldau and Kimberly Patton (eds.), New York: Columbia University Press, 2006, p. 34.

CREATURES OF THE SKY

SIMURGH THE SOUL'S REALITY

The birds of the world set out on a quest to seek their king, who lives beyond the mountain peak of Oaf that has a hundred thousand veils of darkness and light and shines in the light of its own magnificence. Led by their spiritual leader, their murid, a hudhud bird, they travel across seven valleys, expansive seas, and vast deserts, buoyant with joy but weighed down by sighs.

By the end of the pilgrimage, only thirty remain. When these thirty reach their king, the Simurgh, and look upon his radiant face, they see themselves, as though in a mirror. 'What is this mystery?' they want to know. 'We see two: ourselves and ourselves in the mirror; we see both, but the two are one.'

'I am the mirror in front of your eyes,' the Simurgh replies. 'All who come before my splendour see themselves—their own unique reality. You came as thirty, you saw thirty; (si=thirty, murgh=bird). If you had come as forty, you would have seen forty; if you had come as fifty, you would have seen fifty. But know that the journey was Me and the deeds were Mine.'

The Simurgh is the ultimate truth, the divine ipseity. In Farid ud-Din Attar's *Mantiq ut-Tayr* (The Conference of the Birds), the Simurgh is in whom 'the substance of all beings is undone, and they are lost, like shade before the sun'. Thus, beholding the Simurgh is annihilation, and these thirty birds reach fana, an enlightened state in which one's

I-ness is destroyed with the recognition of a fundamental One-ness.

In folklore, the Simurgh is a female bird so big, she can easily carry an elephant. She has the head of a dog, the claws of a lion, and sometimes the face of woman. She is said to have seen the destruction of the world three times over, and, in her hoariness, she has gained enough wisdom and learning to impart to the whole world.

In the Avesta, the Simurgh is Meregho Saena, a word that came to mean 'healer'. It lives in the clouds over the mountains, and it brings life-refreshing rain. It also descends to the earth to wrap good fortune around the houses of those who worship Ahura Mazda. It roosts in Harvisptokhm, the all-seeds tree that stands in the middle of Vourukasha, the heavenly sea. When the Saena takes flight, a thousand shoots emerge from the tree, and when it alights, a thousand shoots break, shedding spores that are geneses of plants and curative for humans.

In Ferdowsi's *Shahnameh*, too, the Simurgh is a healing female bird, who lives on Albroz's mountain peak that reaches up as far as Parveen, the seven-sister constellation. Her nest of ebony and sandalwood is like a palace covered in clouds. When Zal, the albino son of Sam, the ruler of Zabulistan (Sistan), is abandoned by his father, it is the Simurgh that rears him in her nest, giving him tender meat to suckle, instead of milk.

In the Rig Veda, the Simurgh is Shyena, the best ranking, fleet-winged, supreme falcon that brings Manu immortalizing soma of the divine sacrifice. Shyena is the son of Agni, and, sometimes, Agni himself. Shyena is also the falcon shape of the sacrificial altar.

Thus, the Simurgh is fire; it is fertility; it is healing; it is also the soul's reality of Self.

ZIZ THE BIRD OF CHAOS

After six days of Genesis, God created the ziz, a bird that had the power to reverse creation and bring about primordial chaos.

The ziz is so immense that when it flies, its wingspan covers the whole azure, dimming the sun and obstructing its cosmic functions. When it stands with its feet planted in the ocean floor, the waters reach only up to its ankles, and its head touches the sky. Once, it so happened, that sailors crossing the ocean spotted the bird. Seeing that the water was no higher than its ankles, they thought it was shallow enough for them to dive in and enjoy a frolic. Just as they were about to jump off the ship, a thundering, heavenly voice warned them, 'Don't dive here. A carpenter dropped his axe in this spot seven years ago, and it still hasn't reached the bottom.'

The ziz bird does not sit on her eggs to incubate them; the fledglings hatch themselves and crack open their own shells to emerge. Once, a mother ziz birthed a rotten egg and flicked it out of the nest. When it fell, it crushed three hundred cedars under its weight, and its albumen flooded sixty cities.

At the end of time, when the righteous of the world gather for the messianic feast, the ziz will be served to them as a delicacy. They say the flesh of the ziz has a variety of tastes; that is why it is called ziz. But no one really knows what it tastes like. Some say it tastes like this, and others say it tastes like that.

KAKA BHUSUNDI THE TIME-TRAVELLING CROW

There is a purple mountain, Nilagiri; it is far away, north of Mount Sumeru. It has many majestic golden peaks, and on each stands a tree: a banyan, a peepul, a pakara, a mango. On top of the mountain is a lake with jewelled steps, whose water is cool, clear, and sweet. The lotuses in it are abundant and many-hued; and the white-winged swans that throng it are the most elegant. On this mountain lives the immortal Kaka, the crow, Bhusundi. Aeon after aeon, day after day, he meditates under the peepul and sacrifices under the pakara. Then he sits under the banyan and recites episodes from Rama's life. Birds flock to the mountain to listen to his stories, and the swans in the lake draw near the edge of the water to catch every word he speaks.

Once, Shiva, suffering the agony of Sati's self-immolation, also came to the mountain lake in the form of a swan to listen to Kaka Bhusundi. Hearing about Rama's angst at his separation from Sita, the Great God felt comforted.

Garuda, too, went to Nilagiri once, when he was feeling aggrieved at having witnessed Rama suffer the ravages of war that he had to wage against Ravana to rescue Sita. 'How do you know Rama's stories?' Garuda asked Kaka Bhusundi.

'I repeatedly visit Rama's life to experience it, especially his childhood,' Kaka Bhusundi replied. 'I never tire from watching his toddler games, his naughty pranks, and his playful tussles with his brothers. One time, watching the infant Rama, I was baffled: how could the all-knowing Hari be like any other ordinary boy, crawling on his little rosy hands and wobbly knees, smiling with two tiny teeth peeping from between rosebud lips? Rama discerned my perplexity and, one day, when I was visiting his childhood, he showed me with his maya how it is possible.

'That day, after my visit, when I flew off, I noticed that behind me, little Rama had stretched out his arm, as if to catch me. No matter how high I flew, his hand was right there behind me, just two fingers-breadth away. Piercing the universe's seven veils of earth, water, fire, ether, cosmic ego, and cosmic intellect, I attained the utmost height, but even there I saw Rama's arm reaching towards me. Terrified by the marvel, I closed my eyes, and when I opened them again, I found myself in the city of Ayodhya. Here, I came face to face with the adult Rama, and seeing me, he laughed out loud. Suddenly, I was pulled into his open mouth, and he swallowed me. In Rama's belly, I was caught in countless time cycles and innumerable universes with millions of Brahmas, Shivas, and Lokapalas, countless stars, mountains, plains, moons, deaths and births, and beings and creatures of all kinds. I stayed in each universe for a hundred years, and, in each, I saw my own self in Ayodhya, where I beheld the Saranyu River and Rama's parents, Dashratha and Kaushalya, and his brothers, Bharata, Lakshmana, and Shatrughana. In all the universes, I also witnessed Rama's descent on earth and the divine play of his life. Each universe had its own peculiar distinctions; only Rama and his life remained unchanged.

'I was inside Rama only for a fraction of a second, but in that blink of an eye, hundreds of aeons passed by, leaving me utterly bewildered. Noticing my confusion, Rama laughed again, and I flew out of his mouth. Instantly, I found himself back in Ayodhya, where Rama was an infant again, and I had, once again, become a little crow. Caught in the perplexity of this circular time and astounded by the cosmic majesty I had seen in Rama's belly, I lost consciousness. When I regained my senses, I begged the Lord to save me. Rama then ceased the illusion and, placing his lotus hand on my head, removed my sorrows. He also told me to ask for a boon.

'"Let me live in devotion to you forever," I pleaded.

'"So be it," Rama declared. "From today, you will be free from sorrow and delusion, and you will live forever in my bhakti."

'Making that pronouncement, Rama became an infant again and began to wail in affront, as all infants do when they are hungry. His mother, Kaushalya, gathered him in her loving arms and, cooing and cajoling, put him to her breast. I returned to my own retreat in Nilagiri, and, since then, I have been singing Rama's glory, unceasingly,' Kaka Bhusundi told Garuda. 'And these birds and swans come to listen to me.'

'But why are you a crow?' Garuda asked. 'You are so highly evolved, and it is obvious that death has no power over you. Surely, you can take any form you wish. Why a crow?'

Kaka Bhusundi then told Garuda his own story: 'I have lived in many forms, and I can give up any form whenever I wish, but I wish to remain a crow so that I can keep visiting Rama and recounting his life. My first birth was in Kali Yuga, in the yuga of sin. I was born in Ayodhya in the body of a Shudra. But I was a strict devotee of Shiva, abhorring even the mention of any other lord. Once, Ayodhya was hit by a famine, and my life became wretched. Destitute and afflicted, I left that country and came to Ujjain. There, I met a Vedic Brahmin who was also devoted to Shiva, and, out of the kindness of his heart, he took me in as a disciple. However, I remained the arrogant fool that I was. One day, I was sitting in a temple, repeating Shiva's name, when my guru entered. In my arrogance, I did not rise to honour him. My guru let my disrespect pass, but Shiva could not tolerate it. His thunderous voice came from heaven, cursing me: "For remaining rooted to your seat like a python, you will become a snake. You will be the vilest of the vile and crawl into the hollow of some tree in some forest and live there till you die. After that, you will be born ten thousand times."

'When my guru heard this curse, he prostrated himself on the ground and begged the Lord to have pity on me. Pleased with my guru's compassion, the Lord relented. "O Shudra," he said to me, "your awareness will not leave you in any of your births. You were born in Ayodhya, the land of Rama, and by my favour, faith in Rama will spring in your heart, and you will be liberated."

'Driven by Shiva's curse, I went to Vindhya Mountains, and there I took birth as a snake. After that body expired, I was reborn in various forms, but my cognizance never left me. Whatever body I inhabited, whether brute, or divine, or human, I remained devoted to Rama, and I also remembered the kindness of my guru. Finally, I was born as a Brahmin, and even in that form, I remained fixed in Rama and exulted in listening to stories about him. I met many wise men and seers, who told me that God abides in all beings; hence, I should fix my concentration on the impersonal God. But I longed to worship only at the feet of Rama.

'Once, on Mount Meru, I met Rishi Lomasha, and with him, too, I had many debates about the formless God versus God in the form of Rama, and I argued with him endlessly about the superiority of the latter. Finally, tired of my obstinate refusal to perceive the truth of both forms, Rishi Lomasha said to me, "Because you view everything I say with distrust, and because you are so self-opinionated, you will become a crow, a pariah among birds." When I happily accepted this form, Rishi Lomasha realized that for me, the whole world is pervaded only with Rama. He then gave me a Rama mantra and, with that, I am able to see the divine play of Rama forever.'

BYANGOMA AND BYANGOMI

Byangoma and Byangomi are a pair of magical birds in *Thakurmar Jhuli* (Grandmother's Sack of Stories). They have the power of human speech and can foretell the future. They are so miraculous that even their droppings can cure ailments. Humans are always seeking their help, but one must know how to reach them. They nest in banyan trees that grow beyond the seven seas and thirteen rivers.

Dakshinaranjan Mitra Majumdar and Lal Behari Dey captured these birds in their tales. In the story of 'Lalkamal Neelkamal', when the two princes take on the impossible mission of finding rakshasa land, Byangoma and Byangomi fly them on their backs in exchange of a selfless act. In the story of 'Phakir Chand', these birds foretell the death of a prince and then help avert it through the sacrifice of the prince's own newborn infant. In 'Prince Sobur', when the prince's body is pierced with glass, and no one knows how to cure him, it is Byangoma and Byangomi who heal him by smearing their own dung on his body. Hiraman the parrot, also seeks these birds to restore the sight of his king, who is blinded by his rival and can only be cured with a salve of fresh dung from the chicks of Byangoma and Byangomi. Searching for these birds, Hiraman flies beyond the seven seas and thirteen rivers to find the banyan tree in which they nest, and, collecting the dung on a leaf, brings it for the king. The king regains his sight, and lives happily ever after with his new queen.

Byangoma and Byangomi enthralled generation after generation of Bengali children with their human voices. But, today, these magical birds are silent, along with all the other fairy-tale creatures, inside Thakurmar's closed jhuli. No one opens grandmother's sack any more. No one tells these stories.

The fairy tales of the West are what grab the children's attention now. Even the grandmothers themselves have lost touch with our cradle tales.... Gone are the stories of Prince Sabor and the mythical birds, Byangoma and Byangomi. Gone are the tales of jewels and gemstones inherited by seven generations of kings and stashed in lands far away, across seven seas and thirteen rivers.

(Rabindranath Tagore's Introduction to *Thakurmar Jhuli*, 1907)

HIRAMAN THE TALKING PARROT

A Bhil woman once gifted King Sumana of Kanchanapuri a Hiraman parrot called Shastraganja, who, in a human voice, could recite the entirety of the four Vedas. This parrot is a character in Somadeva's *Kathasaritsagara,* and he is also in Banabhatta's *Kadambari,* where his name is Vaishampayana; it is through his human memories that the romance of Chandrapeeda and Kadamabari is revealed.

We also meet the talking parrot in the lyrical poems of the seventh century *Amarushataka* (One Hundred Poems of Amaru). This parrot hears the love talk of a young couple in the night, and, without regard for their privacy, begins to repeat everything in the morning before a roomful of elders. Dying of embarrassment, the young bride shuts its beak by placing in it a ruby, as one would a pomegranate seed.

A talking parrot is the storyteller in the twelfth-century *Shukasaptati* (Seventy Tales of the Parrot), as well. He forestalls Padmavati, the wife of a merchant's son, from taking a lover by narrating a cautionary tale of infidelity every night for seventy nights

In the fourteenth century, this parrot was given a Persian tongue by Ziya' al-Din Nakhshabi in his *Tutinama,* and he tells fifty-two tales to a woman called Khojasta to prevent her from having an adulterous affair, while her husband, Maimunis, is away.

Adept at sexual exposés and an advocate of fidelity, the Hiraman is also a champion of love and romance, especially in the blossoming season of spring, when Kamadeva the god of love rides the parrot. For instance, in Lal Behari Dey's Bengali folktale of the Hiraman, this parrot guides the lovesick king across seven seas and thirteen rivers on Pakshiraj the flying horse to unite him with the princess, for whom he has abandoned all his other wives.

In Malik Muhammad Jayasi's sixteenth-century *Padmavat*, the Hiraman not only becomes a messenger of love but also love's protector, to the extent of sacrificing his own life. Here is that tragic tale:

> Padmavati, the princess of Sinhala, has a golden-bodied Hiramani, whom she loves above all else. The princess and the parrot do everything together, including learning the Vedas. Hiramani becomes so adept at memorizing the Vedic mantras that people begin to hail him as a sage, and Padmavati begins to turn to him for all advice. As Padmavati comes of age, she confides in Hiramani her youthful desires of love and marriage. Hiramani then promises her that he will find her a husband who will be her perfect match. Someone carries this tale to King Gandharvasena, Padmavati's father, to warn him that the parrot is filling his daughter's mind with ideas of love and lust. Enraged, Gandharvasena orders the bird killed. Hiramani escapes, but he is caught by a fowler, who sells him to a Brahmin travelling to Chittor. In Chittor, Hiramani is sold to the monarch, Raja Ratnasena, and, sitting in a cage in the king's bed chamber, he begins to describe Padmavati's beauty to him. Enchanted by the description, Ratnasena embarks on a long journey to Sinhal, crossing the seven seas, disguised as a poor

ascetic, hoping to woo Padmavati and persuade her to marry him. However, both Ratnasena and Padmavati have to suffer many travails before they are united, and, throughout these, Hiramani remains their constant and trusted messenger. Ultimately, Ratnasena weds the Sinhala princess and brings her to Chittor. But in Chittor's court is a tantric scholar, Raghav Chetan, who, turning traitor to the king, goes to Alauddin Khalji in Delhi and extols Padmavati's beauty to him in such a way that Khalji is compelled to acquire her. He attacks Chittor. Ratnasena is killed in battle. And Padmavati commits sati.

Near Chittor is Gagron Fort, and it is believed that this is the habitation of Hiraman parrots. According to legend, when Khalji came to conquer Chittor and abduct the beautiful Padmavati, hundreds of Hiraman in Gagron's forest spoke in the voices of Khalji's men to mislead him. When Khalji discovered the truth, he set the whole forest aflame, and hundreds of Hiraman perished.

The talking parrot is the male of the species. He has a dark pink ring around his nape, which indicates his ability to replicate a human voice. He learns to speak through a natural instinct of imitation, but if one wishes to quicken his talent, one can put him before a mirror and speak from behind. Watching his own reflection and hearing the voice, the parrot thinks he himself is speaking and begins to mimic the sound.

The Hiraman is a native of India, and he is called by different names across the regions: Gangaram, Mian Mithu, Mani, and Kili. For centuries, he has been living in a cage, talking to people, delighting them with his chatter and gossip, feeding on his favourite ghee churi, green chillies, and jaggery. Sometimes, he is also employed by soothsayers, who call upon him to pick fortune-telling cards. Stepping out of his cage, he sifts through the cards and, selecting the prediction, returns behind bars.

Living in captivity for so long, the Hiraman is now almost extinct.

Rumi tells the story of a singing caged parrot in *Masnavi*:

> A merchant in Persia owned him and loved him for his singing voice. Once, this merchant had to go to India for business, and, just before he left, he asked his parrot what gift he desired.
> 'Describe to the parrots there my beautiful cage and remind them of our days of camaraderie, when we flew from one tree to another in freedom,' the parrot said to the merchant. 'Also tell them that as a captive in exile, I long to be with them.'
> Travelling in India, the merchant once came upon a flock of parrots, and, remembering his pet parrot's message, he conveyed it to the birds. Suddenly, one of the parrots shivered and fell down dead. When the merchant returned to his home and told his caged bird about this incident, he also fell off his perch and lay lifeless. Weeping in grief, as the merchant took the dead bird out of the cage, it suddenly came alive in a flutter of wings, and, taking flight, alighted on a nearby tree branch.
> 'Why did you pretend to be dead?' the merchant asked him.
> 'My beautiful voice kept me caged. I have renounced it. And now I am free,' the parrot replied.

'How so?'

The parrot then told the merchant that the Hindustani parrot had only feigned death to convey to him the means of escaping confinement. 'The body is a cage and only in freeing oneself from it resurrection is possible,' he explained.

The merchant realized what the parrot was saying.

JATAYU THE BRAVEHEART

Jatayu was a vulture as big as a mountain. He lived for 60,000 years. He was such a braveheart that, despite his great age, he fought the mighty Ravana in an attempt to stop him from abducting Sita and almost brought down that ten-headed king of Lanka.

Rama and Lakshmana first met Jatayu in the forest near Panchavati, where they had come to spend their fourteen-year exile. They thought the fearsome beast was an asura and pulled out their weapons to fight him. But the vulture spoke to them in gentle tones, telling them about his friendship with their father and his own divine lineage. He was the descendant of Kashyapa, the Saptarishi responsible for the earth, and Tamra, the daughter of Daksha, the progenitor. The couple had five daughters, and each gave birth to a species of birds. Among them was Shyeni, who bore Jatayu and his elder brother, Sampati.

Impressed by the account of Jatayu's forebears, Rama entrusted Sita to his care during their exile. Thus, when Ravana abducted Sita, Jatayu was dharma bound to save her. He was sleeping in a tree when the king of Lanka threw Sita into Pushpaka, his flying chariot. Sita's loud wails, as she called to the trees and rivers of the forest to convey her plight to Rama, awoke Jatayu. He flew into Ravana's path to block him, but Sita begged him to move away. 'He is armed,' she warned. 'You won't be able to withstand him. But please tell Rama.'

Jatayu tried to appeal to Ravana's sense of dharma, berating him for abducting someone else's lawfully wedded wife, but Ravana only mocked his words.

'I have lived sixty thousand years,' Jatayu then declared. 'I am old; you are young and armed with bow and arrow, protected by armour, and mounted on a chariot. Nevertheless, I will not allow you to take away Sita before my eyes. Fight me.'

The two met like a blast in the sky, like two mountains clashing. Ravana shot a volley of sharp arrows, and Jatayu attacked with his mighty talons. Then, with his wings, he broke two of Ravana's bows. He also killed the horses that were pulling the air chariot and smashed the chariot itself. Ravana fell to the ground. But, using his asura maya, he rose up into the sky again, clasping Sita. Jatayu landed on Ravana's ten heads and began goring his back with his beak. Disconcerted by the attack, Ravana let go of Sita and started pounding Jatayu with all his fists, but Jatayu tore off ten of his arms with his talons. They grew back instantly, and, pulling out swords with each of them, Ravana cut off Jatayu's wings. The valorous bird came crashing to the ground. Sita ran to him to help, but Ravana grabbed her by the hair and, rising into the sky once again, swiftly flew to Lanka.

When Rama and Lakshmana, desperately seeking Sita, came upon the bleeding, mortally wounded Jatayu, who lay like a smashed mountain peak, they knelt by his side. With fading breath, Jatayu told them what had happened. 'I saw the king of Lanka headed south,' he said. 'Although my senses are becoming dull, and my vision has become bleary, I can see in the distance a land where trees are made of gold. That is where Ravana has taken Sita, using his conjuring tricks of maya. However, I can also tell you, Rama, that you will certainly destroy that asura and win back Sita.' With these words, the great and brave soul shut his coppery eyes and passed away.

Rama cremated Jatayu with full Vedic rituals, as though he were his own dear parent. And, sprinkling his ashes in the Godavari, bowed to his spirit in utmost respect.

It is believed that the place where Jatayu fell, after Ravana severed his wings, is in Chadayamangalam in Kerala. There, a rock still bears the marks of Jatayu's beak and Rama's footprints. This is where Rama sat with Jatayu's head on his lap.

If one were to visit this rock today, one would be visiting Jatayu Nature Park, where one would see the world's largest bird sculpture and a plaque with a poem, 'In Memory of Jatayu'.

> ...As we stand on this hill
> with heads bowed
> In the memory of that bird
> Who sacrificed himself as a flower offering
> We indeed churn immortality from death[1]

---

[1] Composed in Malayalam by O. N. V. Kurup; translated by K. Jayakumar.

PEACOCK THE BEAUTIFUL, THE SAD

When it rains, the peacock dances. Its train feathers of blue, gold, red, and green, stamped with iridescent ocelli, lift and spread in a fan that shimmers and rustles and quivers.

The peacock's tail used to be just plain blue. Once upon a time, Ravana invaded heaven, and Indra, the king of gods, fearing for his life, hid behind the feathers of the peacock. To show his gratitude, Indra then bestowed on the peacock, a boon: 'Your tail will resemble my thousand eyes. When I shower down rain, you will rejoice.'

The Kutia Kondh tribals believe that the first peacock was created by their creatrix, Goddess Nirantali. Once the goddess was urinating in her garden when a fly came and sat on her private parts. Then, in the mood for some mischief, it flew off and, alighting on an elephant's trunk, described Nirantali's genitalia to him. Then it flew off again, this time into the nose of a tiger. When the tiger sneezed, the fly was hurled out, and it landed in a hole in a tree. In the meantime, an angry Nirantali had sent two men to find the fly. Spotting it in the tree, they cut it down, and catching the fly, brought it the goddess. Nirantali ripped off the fly's cuticle and, extracting the wax, created a tiny little bird from it. Then she stuck small bits of bamboo leaf on the bird's head to make a crest, and, from slivers of bamboo shoot, she fashioned a tail. Finally, taking her silver nose-ring, she crushed it and sprinkled the scraps all over the body of the bird. This was the first peacock.

Considering the peacock's ornate plumage, it is hard to believe that he has ugly legs; they are greyish and scaly. This is because a titihari bird robbed him. Once, the titihari was invited to a wedding feast, and she was in despair, because all she had to wear to the celebration was her own dull, brown coat. So, the titihari went to the peacock and begged him to lend her his beautiful pink legs. He let her borrow them, and she never returned them. That is why, when it rains, the peacock dances in joy, but when he looks down at his ugly legs, he weeps.

In fact, the peacock may be the saddest bird in the world, because it isn't just his legs that cause him grief; he also cannot experience the pleasure of mating. It is believed that his sperm doesn't spill from his generative organ; it spills from his eyes as tears. When he weeps, the peahen drinks his tears to conceive.

The Gond people of Balaghat tell a slightly different story: once, Drupti Mata became angry with the people, and to punish them, she sent diseases upon the crops and cattle. To appease her, a Gond, called Nanga Baiga, created a peacock from the dirt of his body and gifted it to her. He gave the bird everything except a penis. Thus, whenever the dark monsoon clouds cover the sky, the peacock's body fills with sperm. He dances till he tires, and when he coughs with fatigue, his seeds come out of his mouth. The waiting peahen, filled with desire, catches the seed in her beak and swallows it.

The misfortunes of the peacock even transfer to men. The nineteenth century folklorist Marian Roalfe Cox tells the story of how the peacock's eyes became the bane of man's life.

> When God created the peacock, the Seven Deadly Sins
> gazed with envy at the splendid plumage of the bird

and complained of the injustice of the Creator. 'You are quite right; I have been unjust,' said the Creator, 'for I have already bestowed too much on you; the Deadly Sins ought to be black as Night, who covers them with her veil.' And taking the yellow eye of Envy, the red eye of Murder, the green eye of Jealousy, and so on with the rest, he placed them on the feathers of the peacock and gave the bird its liberty. Away went the bird, and the sins, thus despoiled, followed close on his track, trying in vain to recover their lost eyes. This is the reason why, when a man decks himself with a peacock's feathers, the sins incarnate dog his steps and assail him each in its turn.

CHITTA BAAZ

Guru Gobind Singh is called Chitta baaz wallah (one who holds the white falcon). In most images, the Guru is shown with a white falcon perched on his left arm. This bird is, most likely, the northern goshawk, which is Punjab's state bird.

A goshawk is a large bird—about two feet from beak to wingtip, with a wingspan of about a hundred centimetres. Usually, its colour is slate grey, except for an eyebrow-like white stripe over each eye. However, there is a rare variety, known as kufri baaz, which is light grey, morphing to white. But this bird is a native of Siberia; a cold climate bird. Therefore, more than likely, the baaz that the Guru had was not the kufri baaz but the northern goshawk, which was not only a prized hunting bird in Mughal culture, but it was also often presented as a royal gift.

In fact, the reference to the Guru's chitta baaz may not have been to the bird's actual white colour but to what it signified. The Punjabi word, 'chitta' may be a distortion of 'citta', a Sanskrit word that has many meanings, all related to mindfulness and cognizance: thought, reflection, memory, imagination, intelligence, reason, and objective. Islamic mysticism adds another meaning to the significance of the bird: in Sufi poetry, the baaz represents Irji'i—the return of the righteous soul to God—the falcon being the soul and the falconer, God. Thus, the falcon flies off to hunt, engaging with the temporal world, but when the falconer sounds the drum, it returns to his hand, transformed, satisfied. As Rumi says:

> How should the falcon not fly
> back to his king from the hunt
> When from the falconer's drum
> it hears to call: 'Oh, come back'?[2]

This consummate fusion of heart, mind, and soul is what the Guru instilled in his disciples, and this is what the baaz epitomizes. Its physical attributes, too, amplify the symbolism. Its broad wings allow it rapid acceleration, and its long, wedge-shaped, rudder-like tail helps it soar, untiring, for long periods of flight. Its powerful legs and sharp, curved talons and beak give it fierce intention, and its honed eye rivets the pursuit of its prey decisively. These qualities make the baaz a formidable foe. But when it receives the call, it returns to the falconer—content, freed, and at peace.

---

[2]*Look! This is Love, Poems of Rumi,* tr. Annemarie Schimmel, Boston: Shambhala Publications, 1996, p. 76.

THE CHAKOR AND
HIS LOVE AND LONGING

Compared to other, more colourful avian species, the chakor partridge is a rather insignificant looking bird. It has a nondescript light brownish plump body with a greyish breast and blurry, black and white stripes on its flanks. Its only claim to beauty is the band of black that runs across its forehead and eyes and down on either side of its tiny white head, to meet like a garland on its breast.

But who doesn't know the metaphor of this bird? Its unrequited love for the moon is what tragic love stories are all about. On moonlit nights, from rocky slopes, where it roosts, the chakor gazes constantly at the moon, yearning for it. People say that it lives only by drinking the moon's rays. In fact, it is so enamoured that it even swallows fiery embers, thinking them to be drops of moonlight. But, no matter how deeply it loves, it can never unite with the one it loves. That is why mystics and poets use the chakor as a metaphor to describe the agony of love's longing.

GARUDA THE DEVOURER

Some say Garuda symbolizes heaven, others say he symbolizes the soul. In the Rig Veda, he is associated with the gods Agni, Surya, and Vayu. He is the king of birds and the vehicle of Vishnu. He is Suparna, of the beautiful wings; he is Garuda, the devourer of snakes. He is also the one who brought amrita, the elixir of immortality, from heaven to earth.

The Mahabharata tells Garuda's story—a journey befitting an epic hero:

Kadru and Vinata were two sisters married to Rishi Kashyapa, the Saptarishi. One day, Rishi Kashyapa decided to bestow a boon on each of his wives. Kadru, the elder, asked for a thousand splendid snake sons, and the younger, Vinata, asked for just two sons, more splendid than Kadru's. Both sisters birthed eggs: Kadru, a thousand, and Vinata two. After five hundred years of incubation in vessels filled with warm oil, Kadru's one thousand eggs hatched, and a thousand snakes were born. Envious that her sister's sons were already born, Vinata then broke open one of her eggs, and her first son, Aruni, emerged. He was a bird. Born prematurely, his upper body was fully formed, but the lower was just a bloody mass. Angry at his mother for forcing his untimely birth, he cursed her: 'Because you were jealous of your sister, you caused harm to your own son. I curse you that you will be your sister's slave for five hundred years.'

This is how the curse transpired and triggered another curse:

Once Kadru and Vinata placed a wager to guess if the divine horse, Uchchaihshravas, was white or black. The loser was to serve as a slave for the other for five hundred years. Vinata said he was white, and Kadru declared he was black. That night, fearing that she might lose, Kadru commanded her snake sons to braid themselves in the horse's tail so that when the sisters went to look at him, he would appear black. But the snakes refused, unwilling to be a party to her deception. Enraged at her sons for refusing a mother's command, Kadru cursed the snakes, 'May Agni consume you in the snake sacrifice of King Janamejaya of the Pandava race.'

Brahma heard this cruel curse and bemoaned a mother's cold heart, but he did nothing to prevent it. He thought the snakes' virulent poison combined with their great strength and rebellious nature will be too much for the world. With this thought, he let the mother's curse come to fruition. In the meantime, hoping to reverse their fate, the snakes decided to do their mother's bidding and braided themselves in Uchchaihshravas's white tail. Hence, at dawn, when the sisters set out across the primordial ocean to determine who won, they saw that the horse's swishing tail was black. Thus, Vinata became Kadru's slave, as per Aruna's curse. The curse on the snakes, too, took affect, despite their intervention. It was irreversible, and their doom in Janamejaya's sacrifice was inevitable. But that is another story.

When Vinata's second egg hatched, Garuda burst out, blazing like doomsday fire at the end of a yuga, lighting up all the directions with his eyes that were sharp and bright like a flash of lightning. As soon as he was born, he grew to such an immense size that his head pierced the sky, and his roar rolled through the ocean like a tidal wave. When the gods saw this being, who surpassed their combined strength and effulgence, they fled to Brahma.

'Do not fear him,' Brahma said to them. 'He is born to set his mother, Vinata, free and to destroy the snakes.'

But, due to his mother's enslavement, Garuda was born into slavery. His unsurpassable strength and inexhaustible energy served only his snake masters. One day, weary of serving the snakes, Garuda asked them what he could do to liberate himself and his mother.

'Bring us amrita, the elixir of immortality,' the snakes replied.

Consequently, Garuda embarked on a great hero's journey to acquire amrita, which had emerged from the primordial ocean during the Great Churning and was kept in Indra's heaven, safeguarded by two female primeval serpents. Flying thousands of yojanas[3] and conquering all obstacles, Garuda reached heaven and attacked Indra's celestial forces. Defeating the gods, he threw asunder heaven and heavenly order. Then penetrating Indra's palace, he tore apart the ferocious serpents and stole the amrita.

When he was on his way back to earth to hand over the amrita vessel to the snakes, Vishnu stopped him. 'You hold the elixir of immortality in your beak, yet you have not swallowed a drop of it', he said. 'I applaud your selfless resolve. For this I want to grant you a boon. Ask me for anything.'

'I want to stay above you,' Garuda replied. 'And I want

---

[3]Yojana was a measure of distance in ancient India. One yojana is about 13 kilometres.

to be immortal without drinking the ambrosia.'

'Granted,' Vishnu declared. 'You will be on the flag staff of my chariot, always above me, and you will be immortal. Now, I desire a boon from you. I want you to be my vehicle.'

'Be it so.' Garuda replied.

As Garuda flew through the sky, mocking the wind with his speed, Indra hurled a thunderbolt at him. But the divine weapon struck him only as mildly as a needle prick. Garuda laughed in derision and said to Indra, 'Now let me throw one of my feathers. See if you can find its ends.' Then, taking a feather from his wing, he cast it in the sky. It stretched across the great azure, so immeasurable that Indra, even with his thousand eyes, couldn't fathom its length. The creatures of the world, too, saw the feather and declared, 'This bird is Suparna—one with beautiful feathers.'

Watching in awe the marvel of the feather, Indra asked Garuda the limit of his strength.

'With one single feather, I can bear this earth with her mountains, forests, oceans and all the worlds put together; and, also, you.'

'O powerful one, let me be your friend,' the king of gods now said. 'And in the name of friendship I ask you what you intend to do with the amrita?'

'I will give it to the serpents to liberate my mother from slavery,' the great bird replied. 'If you wish, you can have it, but let me first fulfil my purpose. After I hand over the vessel to the snakes, you can descend to earth and take it.'

'That will please me greatly,' Indra said.

'But in return, I want something from you; let the mighty snakes become my food.'

'So be it.'

And, thus, Vinata's bird son became Garuda the devourer of snake.

Descending on earth, Garuda placed the vessel of ambrosia on the sacred kusha grass before the snakes, who had been eagerly awaiting his arrival, dreaming dreams of immortality. 'Here is the amrita,' he said to them. 'I have fulfilled my promise; now liberate my mother.'

'She is free.' the snakes declared, excitedly slithering towards the amrita.

'Wait!' Garuda called. 'Don't you think that you should bathe and purify yourself before you drink this divine elixir?'

The snakes stopped in their tracks and then sped towards the river.

Just at that moment, Indra swooped down from heaven and whisked the vessel away. When the snakes returned from their ablutions, they saw the kusha grass but no amrita. It was gone. All that remained of it was a few drops that had spilled on the kusha grass when Garuda had placed the vessel on it. They knew they had been duped, but there was nothing they could do. They licked the drops of amrita from the grass, and the spiky sharp kusha blades split their tongues in half.

Popular belief says that Garuda spilled amrita on earth even prior to this incident. When the Great Ocean was churned, and, Dhanvantri, the physician of the gods, arose from it, carrying a kumbha (vessel) of amrita, the task of transporting the vessel to heaven was given to Garuda. On his way there, the Great Bird accidentally spilled a few drops in four different spots—Prayag, Haridwar, Nasik, and Ujjain. Hence, these became river pilgrimages, and the Kumbha Mela is celebrated in these places every twelve years.

Being the enemy of snakes and the transporter of amrita,

Garuda is invoked in antidotal mantras to cure snakebite. Brahma taught these mantras to Narada, and they were compiled in the Garuda Upanishad. This is how they became known in the world, and this is how Garuda came to be recognized as the knower of life and death and the keeper of the secret of immortality.

Once, sitting at ease in Vishnu's abode, Vaikuntha, Garuda requested the Great Lord to tell him about Yama, the lord of death, and also about the sins of men and the hells they have to suffer for those sins.

'When a man is dying, ferocious yellow and black messengers of Yama, bearing nooses and rods, come to him. They are naked and grinding their teeth, their hair is erect, their faces are ugly, and their nails are like weapons. Seeing them advance, the dying man's heart palpitates, and he releases excrements. Yama's servants drag the man from his body, and he emerges, no bigger than the size of a thumb. Looking down at his dead body, he cries out, "Oh! Oh!"

'As the soul crosses the Vaitarani River, which extends a hundred yojanas and lies between earth and Yamaloka, the righteous one sees it filled with amrita and crosses it with ease. But for the sinner, it is full of pus and blood, malodorous, and obstructed with hairy moss. It is also swarming with huge crocodiles and crowded with hundreds of dreadful birds, and on its banks are heaps of bones and mounds of rotting flesh. When the river sees the sinful approach, it emits flames and smoke, and it seethes, like butter in a heated pan. A monstrous throng of insects with piercing stings and immense vultures and crows with adamantine beaks attack the sinful soul, while porpoises, crocodiles, leeches, and other flesh-eating water-vermin threaten to devour him...'

This conversation between Garuda and Vishnu about the path of the soul and the twenty-eight hells is described in the Garuda Purana. The recital of this Purana during funerary rites at a person's death allows relatives to help alleviate the tortures of hell for the departed soul.

Thus, the immortal Garuda, the vehicle of Vishnu, becomes a vehicle for people to learn the truth about the transmigration of the soul.

PHOENIX—REBORN FROM ITS OWN ASHES

In the Garden of Eden, when the serpent offered Eve the forbidden fruit from the Tree of Knowledge, Eve shared it with the animals. They all ate it. The only one who refused was the phoenix bird. Hence, Yahweh bestowed on the phoenix immortality; and thus it was that when God created the Angel of Death, he had dominion over all creatures except the phoenix.

Baruch ben Neriah, who was the scribe and disciple of Prophet Jeremiah of the Hebrew Bible, was once taken by an angel to the region of the sun. There, he saw the mountain-sized phoenix, along with the rainbow hued chalkydri, pulling the chariot of the sun. The angel told Baruch that the phoenix flies alongside the sun with its wings spread wide so that it can deflect the sun's fiery rays, or else, the creatures of the earth will be scorched to death. On the open wings of the phoenix, Baruch saw written: 'The earth has not borne me, nor has heaven. I am borne by wings of fire.'

At dawn, when the angels open the 365 gates of heaven, the phoenix rouses the roosters on earth so that they can awaken humanity. Throughout the day, men's lawless and unrighteous actions defile the sun, and by dusk, its rays are diminished. Then the phoenix, too, withdraws its wings, exhausted and spent from restraining the sun's fire all day. It rests all night, and, at daybreak the next morning, it resumes its task again.

The phoenix eats manna from heaven and, drinks the

dew of the earth. It lives a thousand years, and as the years pass, it grows smaller and smaller, until it is no bigger than a fledging. Soon, its wings fall off, and a fire arises from its nest. And the phoenix bursts into flames. Then God sends two angels to reconstruct the egg from which the bird first hatched, and a new phoenix emerges. It instantly grows to its full size to live another thousand years.

The inspiration for the Christian and Judaic phoenix were Greek and Roman myths, which were, probably, inspired by the Egyptian Bennu heron that was believed to be self-created and Ra, or soul of the sun god. Iso, like the sun, experienced continual death and rebirth. The phoenix that the Greek historian, Herodotus, describes is eagle-like and as brilliant as the sun, with feathers of red and gold. It buries its father every five hundred years in the temple of the sun in an egg made of myrrh. However, according to Pliny, the Roman philosopher, the phoenix burns itself in a nest of cinnamon, and a new phoenix is born from the bones of the old. Many Roman emperors used the phoenix as a symbol to emblemize the Roman empire and their own undying power. Later, Christians adopted the phoenix as a metaphor of Christ's Resurrection.

Apollonius, the second century Greek philosopher, too, describes the phoenix as a shining golden eagle, emitting rays of sunlight, sitting in its nest at the springs of the Nile. When it begins to be consumed by flames, it sings its own requiem. He says, the phoenix visits Egypt every five hundred years, but it is a native of India.[4]

---

[4] *The Life of Apollonius of Tyana*, Philostratus, Book 3, Ch. 49, tr. F. C. Conybeare, 1912, Internet Sacred Texts Archive.

CREATURES
OF THE
SEA

MATSYA THE COSMIC FISH

In the beginning, Matsya was so small, it could be kept in a jar; then it grew so large, even the Ganga could not contain it. Glistening like moonbeams in the water, Matsya pulled Manu's ship out of the cosmic flood of dissolution so that he could help recreate the world. From fish to Brahma to Vishnu's first avatar, Matsya has been a saviour in every aeon.

The Shatapatha Brahmana describes an encounter that Manu, the progenitor, had with a tiny fish one morning when he was washing his hands in a tank. The fish leapt into his hands and said, 'Rear me, I will save you.'

'From what will you save me?' Manu asked.

'There will be a great flood, and it will carry away all the creatures. I will save you from this flood.'

'How should I rear you?' Manu then asked.

'You should keep me in a jar. When I outgrow that, dig a pit to make a pond and keep me in it. When I outgrow that, take me down to the sea, because then I will be beyond destruction. Big fish eat little ones; as long as they are little, they are always in danger of being devoured.'

From a little fish, it soon became a ghasha (a large fish); and then it grew to be the largest of all fish. Once, it said to Manu, 'In such and such a year, that flood will come. Build a boat, and when the water has risen, climb into it, and I will save you.'

When the fish became immense, Manu took it to the sea. Then, the time which the fish had predicted, arrived and a flood occurred. Manu built a boat, and when the waters rose, he climbed into it. The fish swam up to the bow so that Manu could tie the boat's rope to its massive horn, and it pulled the vessel to the northern mountain. 'I have saved you,' it said. 'Fasten the boat to a tree and watch the water. When it subsides, slowly descend the mountain.'

All creatures were swept away in the rising waters; Manu alone survived. And when the cosmic flood receded, he came down from the northern mountain. Then, desiring offspring, he engaged in austerities and performed sacrifices, offering clarified butter, sour milk, whey, and curds in the water. After a year, a woman, Ida, was born from these offerings. She was Manu's daughter, because he had birthed her from his consecration, and with her as sacrifice, Manu generated his own race.

◆

In the Mahabharata, the cosmic fish is not just a fish; it is Brahma the Creator, and Manu is Manu Vaivasvata, the father of Ila and Ikshvaku, from whom both the lunar and solar dynasties came to be. Thus, he is the progenitor of manavas (human beings). Here is the tale from the Mahabharata:

Once Manu, wearing nothing but bark, sat in meditation on the bank of River Vaitarani, which flows between the mortal world and Yamaloka, the region of death. After Manu had meditated for ten thousand years, a fish came swimming up to him and begged him to save it from the big fish, promising in return to do a good deed for Manu. Feeling compassion, Manu gathered the fish in his hands and put it in a jar. As in the earlier tale, the fish grew so much that Manu had to move it from the jar to a pond, and from there to the river Ganga. And, when the Ganga became too cramped for it, Manu took it to the ocean.

'You have given me protection, now listen to what I have to tell you,' the fish said to Manu. 'When the time to cleanse the world comes and everything mobile and immobile on earth is destroyed, build a sturdy boat and, taking the seven Great Rishis with you, climb into it. Also carry with you the seeds of all the creatures.'

As soon as the flood came, Manu gathered the seven seers in the boat and brought with him the seeds of all the creatures. When the ocean began to billow and all signs of earth disappeared, the fish swam up to the boat, its horn raised above the water like a mountain. Manu looped a rope around that horn, and the fish pulled the boat to the highest point of the Himalaya. Then the fish declared to Manu, 'I am Brahma the Lord of Creatures. In the form of a fish, I have set you free from danger. You should now create all creatures from the seeds you have brought with you—gods, asuras, men, and others that stir and do not stir.'

◆

In the Matsya Purana, Manu himself asks Brahma for a boon to make him the protector of all creatures at the time of dissolution. Here, the fish becomes Vishnu's first avatar, Matsya:

Once when Manu was performing a water ritual in his hermitage, a restless little saphari fish with beautiful eyes came into his hands. He put it in a vessel, and when it became sixteen fingers long and begged him to save it, Manu put it in a jar. It grew three hands in one night, and Manu transferred it to a lake. After that, he took it to the Ganga, and from there to the ocean. When it kept growing and filled the whole ocean, Manu became frightened. 'Who are you?' he asked the fish. 'Are you an asura full of maya? Or are you Vasudeva? You have become twenty thousands leagues from a small saphari. Who else is capable of this, except Keshava?'

'Yes, it is I,' Vishnu said. 'You have recognized me.' Then, Matsya, the fish avatar of Vishnu, told Manu about the impending destruction of the world and instructed him that when the great flood comes, he should put all creatures in a boat. 'I will then pull your boat to safety,' Vishnu said. 'You will be the progenitor at the beginning of Krita Yuga, the overlord of the period of Manu.'

(In this variant of the tale, Manu is curious to know how long the period of destruction will last, and by what means will he protect all creatures.)

'There will be a drought on earth that will last a hundred years, and people will die; those remaining will be burnt by seven ordinary rays of the sun that will become seven times more powerful and will fall like hot coals. Then the submarine mare that emitted from Shiva's third eye will open her mouth, spewing flames. A poisonous fire will also shoot out from the mouth of Shesha Naag, on whose head the world rests. Then, from Shiva's third eye, the fire of dissolution will emanate, and the three worlds will be burnt to ashes. When everything is annihilated, seven clouds will form from the sweat of Agni and pour down rain, flooding the earth. Ultimately, all the waters will unite and flow as one, and the earth will be submerged. At that time, you should get a boat and put the Vedas in it. Also place in it the seeds of creation. Fasten the boat to my horn, and I will take you to safety.'

When the time came, Vishnu, in the form of the horned fish, Matsya, came to Manu, bringing with him a serpent that Manu used as rope to tie the boat to the fish.

In time, Manu, the great progenitor and the protector of all mankind, rebirthed the world with the help of the cosmic fish. At the beginning of this new creation, Vishnu once again propagated the Vedas, and a new age began.

LEVIATHAN THE SEA MONSTER

The Leviathan may have been a colossal crocodile or, perhaps, a whale-like beast that once existed. In the Old Testament, it is a twisting, writhing, seven-headed, monstrous sea serpent of the deep that is so gigantic, it encircles the whole world, and no man can harness it. Its arched jaws are a thing of terror, and its body is covered with scaly shields that are enclosed so tightly within clamped walls of flint that not even air can pass through them. Its eyes gleam like the shimmer of dawn, and firebrands shoot from its mouth. When it breathes, sparks fly, and its nostrils pour out smoke. Its breath is so fiery, it sets coals ablaze, and the deep water is blown to full heat, like a cauldron set on a flame. When it shifts its head, the sinews of its neck create dancing waves of energy around it, and when it raises itself, strong men take flight, bewildered at the lashings of its tail. Its underbelly is unyielding, and its heart is as firm as the nether millstone. No sword, no spear, no javelin can cut it. Iron is like straw before it, and bronze is rotting wood. No arrow can pierce it, and sling stones are turned to chaff. A club is like a reed for it, and it laughs at the swish of a sabre. Whenever it ambles through the waters, it leaves a shining trail behind, making the great river appear like a white hair in its wake.

It is king over all proud beasts—this creature of chaos.

According to *Midrash*, the Leviathan was created on the fifth day. Initially, God created a pair—a male and female

Leviathan—just as he created all other creatures. But then he thought about their offspring and the combined strength they would inherit; what havoc they could bring with it. Hence, God killed the female and castrated the male. Other sources say that the Leviathan was created female, and she lives in the seas, while a land monster, the Behemoth, was created male.

At the end of time, when the Messiah comes, God will kill this sea serpent, this beast equated to chaos, and serve its flesh at the banquet for the righteous. From its scaled hide God will make tents for the pious of the first rank, girdles for those of the second, chains for those of the third, and necklaces for those of the fourth. Then, taking the remainder of the hide, he will spread it on the walls of Jerusalem, and the whole world will be illuminated by its brightness. Until then, God will treat the Leviathan as his plaything.

MAKARA THE IMMORTAL CROCODILE

Makara is the ancestor of all Indian species of crocodiles: magarmaccha, the marsh and saltwater crocodiles, and gharial, the long-snouted, river inhabitant. Makara is also the leitmotif in many Indic traditions.

Most ancient Indian art depicts Makara as a short, squat, dragon-like creature that has a marsh crocodile's head and a small, slightly open snout that displays sharp pointed teeth. Its body is scaly, and it has a tail of either a crocodile or a fish; its ears are tiny and pointed, like a hound's, and it has four stubby legs. Sometimes, instead of a crocodile's head and snout, it is shown with the head of an elephant and a raised trunk.

The Makara was a sacred creature in the water cosmology of pre-Vedic times, because it exists on the limen of earth and water. Later, when Varuna became the supreme lord, and his waters became the essence of the universe, the Makara was seen as the essence in the waters: 'rasa in its various equivalents, sap, semen, Water of Life,'[5] as the art historian Ananda K. Coomaraswamy says. That is why Varuna's vehicle was Makara, and it was everything vegetal and everything virile. It is no wonder then that in later myths, Makara became the emblem of Kamadeva, the fecund god of sexual desire.

Kamadeva is also privy to secrets of both death and immortality because he was burnt to ashes by Shiva and then

---

[5] Ananda K. Coomaraswamy, *Yakshas*, part 2, Washington D. C.: Smithsonian Institution, Freer Gallery of Art, 1931, p. 55.

resurrected. And so it is that the Makara, too, signifies this juxtaposition of existence and becomes an apt vehicle for deities of death and afterlife: hence, Yama, the lord of death, and Ganga, the river that accepts the dead and delivers souls, both ride the Makara. Sometimes, especially in Navagraha descriptions, Chandra, the moon, who possesses soma, the elixir of immortality, also sits on Makara.

In addition to its eschatological connections, Makara is associated with prosperity. It is one of the nine guardians of the subterranean treasures of Kubera the lord of wealth. Often, in ancient sculptures, it is shown with a garland of pearls hanging from its mouth, as though challenging the valiant to pluck it from its ferocious jaws. Perhaps, for the early sea traders, who encountered these terrible ship-wreckers in the waters, every safe and profitable sea journey was, indeed, like picking pearls from the jaws of the crocodile. There is, in fact, evidence that the Indus Valley traders propitiated this fearful lord of waters; seals from Mohenjo-daro show prows of boats shaped like Makaras.

In epic times, Makara entered the battlefield. Kautilya's *Arthashastra* mentions an almost impregnable battle formation called the Makara vhuya. In the Mahabharata, Bhishma uses this formation on the fifth day of battle to hold off the Pandavas. Its mouth is clenched so tightly with warriors that only Bhima, with his strength of ten thousand elephants, can penetrate it. On the sixth day, the Pandavas themselves create the Makara vyuha to confound Duryodhana.

Because so much of Indian culture is infused by the Makara, it is prolific in ancient art and sculpture. Hindu temples and sacred caves often had guardian crocodiles carved at the base, entryways, and doorways that were thresholds to the sanctum sanctorum. Sometimes, Makara sculptures also appeared on the outside of sanctum walls as pranalas or waterspouts, from which milk and water offerings pour out. For instance, in Konark, a Makara pranala is still intact outside the Mayadevi temple. But in this Sun temple, another attribute is added to the Makara's repertoire: Makara is also Capricorn, the tenth astrological sign of the zodiac. On the day that the sun enters the constellation Makara, it marks the end of the winter solstice and the first day of the sun's northward transit. This is the beginning of Uttarayanam, the auspicious half of the year that Hindus celebrate as Makara Sankranti, the day of bountiful harvest. Even today, thousands gather in Konarak to observe this propitious occurrence.

In Jyotisha, Makara Rashi is in the Sharavana nakshatra (lunar mansion), and its chief deity is Vishnu. The symbol of this nakshatra is 'ear' because it represents 'listening', which leads to learning, wisdom, and knowledge. Hence the great gods, Vishnu and Shiva are often shown wearing makara kundalas—makara earrings. In fact, the Makara has been a motif in Indian jewellery from the time of the Indus Valley. Even today, a bride's gold bracelet ends are designed with Makara heads to signify that she brings prudence, prosperity, and fecundity into her house of marriage.

KURMA THE WORLD TORTOISE

Kurma the tortoise existed even before Prajapati, the primogenitor of the world. In the beginning, Prajapati alone came into existence on a lotus leaf. When he felt desire in his mind, he said, 'Let me bring forth the universe.' And to do so, he performed austere penances, after which, he shook his body. From his flesh, red rays emitted; from his nails and hair, clans of rishis leapt out; and from his bodily fluids, strange, demonic beings formed. Just then, he saw a tortoise moving in the middle of the water, and he said to him, 'You, too, have come into being from my skin and flesh.'

'No,' the tortoise replied. 'I have been here before you. I am Purusha, the primordial man of a thousand heads, thousand eyes, thousand feet.'

Prajapati realized that the tortoise was, indeed, born before him, and he said, 'All that is svayambhu—self-born—is Brahmana, the ultimate reality.

In the Shatapatha Brahmana, Kurma is Prajapati himself, who brings forth all creatures. Whatever he created, he himself made, and because he made it, he is called Kurma. Rishi Kashyapa, the Saptarishi, one of seven progenitors of the world, is also kachhapa—Kurma; from him came the Adityas, who are the solar gods, and the daityas and danavas, who are forces of darkness, and the mortals, who are his progeny.

Kurma is also Vishnu. When the gods needed to churn the Great Ocean to acquire soma, the elixir of immortality, they begged Vishnu for help. Vishnu took the avatar of Kurma and became the churning base to bear the weight of the grinding, swirling churning stick of Mount Mandar, which rises eleven thousand yojanas upwards and plunges eleven thousand yojanas downwards.

According to Vaastu Shastra, this kurmashila, the tortoise foundation, is stability. That is why at the beginning of Vaastu puja a Kurma image is placed in a lotus that sits on a water pot. A metal tortoise is also buried at the base when the foundation of a house is laid. Temple pillars, too, rest on the backs of tortoise sculptures.

Kurma's lower shell is the terrestrial world, fixed like the earth; its upper shell is the sky, which spreads over the earth, rounded at the ends, and in between the shells is air. Hence, Kurma is the microcosm of the world, and because the world is produced from sacrifice, Kurma is the foundation of the sacrificial altar.

Thus it is that Kurma is the world tortoise, Akupara—boundless, yet fixed, holding the earth stable. And, thus it is that Kurma, the kachhapa, is also an allegory of a person who is steadfast in his quest for realization—one who is able to withdraw his sense organs, just as the tortoise draws its limbs within the shell; one who is firmly fixed, but one whose consciousness is limitless.

TIMINGILA THAT ONCE WAS

There is not much known about timingila, except that it used to be a sea creature so large that it could swallow a whale in one gulp. Its existence was known till epic times, and epical heroes on their journeys saw it drifting in the water, like a great big mass, at least eight miles long.

Arjuna, the Mahabharata hero, saw the creature once, when he was on his mission to find divine weapons for the Great War. Standing on the ocean shore, he saw tortoises and crocodiles in the heaving waves and, floating among them, like gargantuan rocks submerged in water, were timingilas.

Rama and his army of monkeys also witnessed the creature in the shoreless sea. After Hanuman returned from Lanka with news of Sita's captivity in Ravana's Ashoka Vatika, Rama marched his forces across rivers and mountains to the southern shore at the base of Mahendra Mountain, beyond which was a vast stretch of water, whose other end was Lanka. In the giant waves, they saw alligators and whales and the terrible timingilas that could swallow all the other creatures of the sea, including serpents with flaming hoods. But immense though these beings were, the wind gusts were bigger; they thrust the waves with such tremendous force that even these mammoths were tossed about.

To seek safe passage across this mighty ocean, Rama propitiated Varuna, the lord of waters, by sitting on kusha grass for three nights and praying to him. But Varuna remained unmoved. Angered by the arrogance of the god of waters, Rama stood up in resolve. 'Watch me split apart these great sea creatures,' he said to Lakshmana and shot a volley of arrows in the water. Then, mounting on his bow a missile presided over by Brahma, he warned Varuna: 'Today I will dry your waters till all that remains of your domain is sand.'

Even as he pulled the string of his bow, a great cry arose from the sea creatures as they were tumultuously tossed onto the beach like deluge. A fearful Varuna then manifested himself and stood before Rama with folded hands. 'I will allow Nala, the son of Vishvakarma, to build a bridge across the ocean,' he said. 'And I promise that while the monkey army is crossing, my creatures—serpents, alligators, and the massive timingilas, whose natural instinct is to devour—will refrain from harming them.' Thus, due to Varuna's promise, Rama's army of monkeys was able to cross the ocean free of fear, even though they could see the colossal creatures watching them from the waters below.

In fact, the timingila fish was so feared for its size and ingurgitation that it came to represent the unfathomable—a metaphor for poets and writers. For instance, this is how Sri Chaitanya Mahaprabhu described the suffering of gopis when Krishna parted from them: 'The gopis are drowning in an ocean of separation. So great is their pain, it is as though they are being devoured by the timingila.'

VARAHA THE GOOD AND EVIL BOAR

Varaha was a mighty boar who lifted the earth from the cosmic waters.

The Vayu Purana describes Varaha thus: eyes like the lotus, body as vast as Nila Mountain, colour as dark as lotus leaves. Ten yojanas in width, and a thousand yojanas in height, he covers the space between the earth and the sky. He blazes like the sun, and his tusks shine white and sharp, like lightning. His roar is thunderous and frightening, and his mane is so fiery and awesome that it strikes fear even in the heart of Varuna, god of the waters. He strides like a powerful lion; his haunches are fat, his loins slender, and his body is smooth and beautiful.

The Bhagavata Purana says Varaha issued from Brahma's nostrils. When he was born, he was no bigger than a thumb, but he rapidly increased to the size of an elephant and then became as large as a mountain. The Vishnu Purana narrates the cause of why Varaha came to be. When Brahma awakened from his night of sleep and beheld the void resulting from the dissolution of the universe, he saw the earth lying below the waters. To uplift her, he assumed the form of a boar. Seeing him thus, Vasundhara, the goddess Earth, praised him by equating him to sacrifice, oblation, sacrificial fire, and the Vedas. She called him Omkara, the sun, the planets, and the whole world—all that is formless and all that has form; all that is visible and all that is invisible. 'You are Hari, the object of all worship,' she said. 'Elevate me from this place, as you have done in many pasts.'

The Boar took the Earth on his mighty tusks and lifted her up. As he reared his head, the waters shedding from his brow purified the great sages, and the indentations of his hoofs created lower worlds into which the water rushed with a thunderous roar. Rising from the waters, trembling, dripping, he placed Earth on the summit of the ocean and divided her into four spheres: earth, sky, heaven, and the fourth for the sages, that was further apportioned into mountains. Since then, Earth has been floating like a mighty vessel, never sinking.

But Brahma is only the instrumental cause of creation; all things become created as a result of their own material cause; imperceptible substance becoming perceptible according to its own imbued powers. When Brahma lost his supremacy to Vishnu, that Great God came to be seen as the supreme cause and effect of all things, and Varaha, too, came to be regarded as Vishnu's third avatar. However, even Vishnu suffered degradation in the evolving Shakta traditions of the Kalika Purana.

In Kalika Purana, Vishnu's avatar of the Boar is an uncontrollable beast, to whom Shiva says, 'Now that you have fulfilled the purpose of uplifting the earth, you should abandon this powerful body (of the boar), because the earth cannot bear you and is sinking in the water.'

But, instead, the Boar violates Earth while she is in the form of a woman and menstruating, and she becomes pregnant with an embryo of demonic nature. The child she is carrying is Naraka. Recognizing the shamefulness of his act, Vishnu promises Shiva that he will abandon the body of the lustful Boar. But then he escapes to Loka–Aloka Mountains and continues to copulate with Earth, who has taken the form of a female boar. She bears three more sons, Suvratta, Kanaka, and Ghora. The Boar family then gambols across the earth, and in their boisterous frolic, they crack her, and she breaks into two. The Boars also press upon the world serpent, Ananta, which makes him tread upon the world tortoise, Kurma, causing him to stagger. This shatters the tablelands of Mount Meru, and the debris that dismantles makes all the lakes murky. As the Boars sport in the waters, gems get strewn here and there, and wishing trees are torn asunder. The ocean floods, and a deluge threatens the three worlds. Then, the Boar and his family go to heaven, where they destroy Indra's gardens and frighten the gods.

In all this time, although Prithvi, the earth goddess, is unstable and deeply unhappy, her boar form exhilarates in the company of her husband. The Boar, too, as Vishnu's avatar, regrets the destruction he is causing, but in his boar form, he exults in desire which surges unrestrained.

When the gods beg Vishnu to abandon the Boar's form, he says, 'I do want to abandon this body for the sake of all creatures,' and he requests Shankar to slay the Boar. Shiva then assumes the terrible form of Sharabha, which he had taken once before to control Vishnu's Narasimha avatar. A great battle ensues between the Boar and his sons and Sharabha. As they rise, battling, into the sky, heaven shatters, planets are dislodged, mountains fall into the ocean, the waters swell, and the earth splits.

Although he fights fiercely, Sharabha is unable to destroy the boars. Disheartened, the gods once again go to Vishnu and warn him that if he does not withdraw himself from the Boar and absorb his energy, he would have to witness the world, that he himself has created, utterly wrecked. Vishnu then takes the body of a red fish, such as that of Matsya, who had hauled Manu's ship from the Great Flood, and seeing himself transform into this avatar of a Deliverer, Vishnu finally regains the Varaha sensibility. He then recalls his Narasimha avatar, and, as soon as that man-lion becomes present, Varaha draws into himself the energies of both these former avatars. The combined energy of deliverance is so powerful that the Boar cannot contain it, and it emerges like the sun and rises into the sky. Devoid of vital force, the Boar begs Sharabha: 'Kill me in a sacrifice; also perform a sacrifice for each of my sons.'

The sacrifice of the Boar releases his energy, and, shining like a garland of flames lit with ten million suns, it enters Vishnu's body. The sacrifice of Suvratta, Kanaka, and Ghora also releases their force, which Shiva absorbs into himself. Then Sharabha hurls the boars' bodies into the water, which blazes and roars like a doomsday fire and extinguishes them.

Vishnu and Brahma and all the gods approve and say, 'Om'.

THE GOLDEN HAMSA

Hamsa is life breath; it is prana: inhalation 'ham' and exhalation 'sa'. Ham-sa, ham-sa, continually, in all bodies, filling them as completely as fire in fuel, or oil in sesame. He who knows this, holds death at bay. This is what the Hamsa Upanishad says. The Shvetashvatara Upanishad says Hamsa is deathlessness—the Supreme Self that alone exists in this universe: 'He, who, as fire, abides in the water. Only by knowing Him does one pass over death and achieve Moksha.' In the Brihadaranyaka Upanishad, Hamsa is atma—the immortal soul. 'Preserving with breath the ignoble nest (the body), he roams; wherever he likes, he goes; he, the immortal, the golden person, the solitary Hamsa.'

In yoga, Hamsa is jiva, the individual self that, propelled by breath, concentration, and stillness, must transcend through the chakras to the thousand-petalled lotus of the head, where supreme realization resides. Hamsa carries the nectar of bliss from the lower chakras to the lotus in the cranium and releases it in a thousand streams. Ham-sa is then aham (I) and sa (He)—I am He. This realization of oneness makes the yogi a paramhamsa, the supreme Hamsa.

The thousand petals are also the Buddha's ushnisa, the oval protuberance at the top of his head. This is the point of realization, which the Buddha achieves through hamsa-like control. In Gandhara art, the Buddha has webs between the digits of his hands and feet, like a hamsa bird. Just like a Hamsa controls its movement in the water with his webbed feet, so does the Buddha control his actions in the world. And when he soars, he becomes Nirvana.

◆

The Ramayana makes the hamsa bird a divine ancestor, an offspring of Rishi Kashyapa, who was one of the seven progenitorial holy rishis, and Tamra, the daughter of Daksha, who is the son of Brahma. From the union of Kashyapa and Tamra were born five daughters, among whom was Shyeni, who birthed swans and kalahamsa (black hamsa) birds. Being divine, hamsa birds live in Manasarovara, the pure and salvational lake in the Himalayas that Brahma created in his mind, before it became manifest at the base of Shiva's abode, Kailasha.

The kalahamsa became white due to a boon it received from Varuna, the lord of waters: once, King Marutta celebrated the Maheshvara Sattra, an extended sacrifice to propitiate Shiva, and he invited the gods to receive their share of the oblations. At that time, Ravana was on a victory tour, and, learning about this opportune congregation of gods, he arrived at the yajna site to destroy them. Fearing him, the gods hid themselves in the forms of different birds and animals: Indra hid in the peacock, Yama in the crow, Kubera in the chameleon, and Varuna in the kalahamsa. Thus, the gods were able to escape Ravana, and, in gratitude, they bestowed boons on the birds and animals that had concealed them. Indra conferred on the peacock plumage that displayed his own thousand eyes. Yama promised the crow a share of the offering people on earth give to their dead ancestors. Kubera granted the chameleon the ability to change its colour at will. And Varuna made the black hamsa pure white.

Pure white hamsa birds are also messengers of love. In the Nala and Damayanti tale, a Hamsa causes the burgeoning of love between the unknowing Nala and Damayanti. And in the romance of Pururavas and Urvashi, it is in the form of a white hamsa that Urvashi conveys to Pururavas the affirmation of her love.

Hamsas eat pearls, says the Guru Granth Sahib, and they sift water from milk to drink only the milk. Their sense of discernment is the reason why Sarasvati, the goddess of knowledge, rides the Hamsa.

When a Hamsa has achieved realization, it becomes golden.

BADAVA THE SUBMARINE MARE

There is a mare at the bottom of the ocean that is created from the fire banked in the seabed. At the end of the world, at the time of dissolution, she will ignite, and her raging flames will consume the world. This submarine mare is the fire of Shiva's suppressed fury and sexual energy.

Once, the gods were threatened by Tarakasura, an asura who had become indestructible. Only a child born from the union of Shiva and Parvati was ordained to be the saviour. But therein lay the problem: at that time, Shiva was completely oblivious to Parvati's existence. After Sati's self-immolation, he had detached from all worldly desires, withdrawn into himself, and gone into deep meditation. The gods managed to employ the beautiful, maiden Parvati in his service on Himalaya's peak, but the Great God did not even notice her. To break Shiva's concentration and to evoke desire in him for Parvati, the gods summoned Kamadeva, the god of desire.

Accompanied by his wife, Rati, and his companion Vasanta, who is the season of spring, Kamadeva went to Kailasha, carrying his five flowered arrows of desire and his flowery bow, whose string is made of bees. Arriving in Shiva's abode, Kama first had Vasanta spread the enchantment of spring all around the grove where the Great God was seated. When, suddenly, mango and ashoka trees began to bloom, water lilies became abuzz with bees, and cuckoos started cooing, and Shiva's mind registered the untimely arrival of spring, but he continued in penance. Kama then took his mango blossom arrow of joy, Harshana, and mounted it on his bow. Just then Parvati arrived on the scene, carrying a platter of flowers and wearing a single garment that barely concealed her body. That very moment, Shiva opened his eyes and looked at Parvati, and, in that flash of time, Kamadeva pulled the string of his bow. Instantly, Shiva was filled with the intoxication of Parvati's moon-like face, lotus eyes, red bimba-fruit lips, and curvaceous waist.

Restraining his agitated mind, Shiva wondered how he had lost his concentration. When he looked around, he spotted Kamadeva, whose bow was still drawn. Shiva's mind filled with rage, but, in that instant, Kamadeva's bow was already releasing the arrow. Harshana pierced Shiva's breast, but it was futile. Shiva's anger rendered it powerless. Realizing that his arrow had lost its purpose, Kamadeva began to tremble in fear of the Great God's fury.

A terrible flame shot out of Shiva's forehead, its blaze as though of final dissolution. It surged up into the sky and then spread across the earth, consuming everything. Kamadeva was instantly burnt to ashes.

By this time, the gods had also arrived, but they could do nothing. They sent the frightened Parvati to her palace with her maids. But, poor Rati! Seeing her husband reduced to ashes, she fell down in a faint, and when she regained consciousness, all she could do was lament.

'Take heart, dear lady,' the gods consoled her. 'We will beg the Lord to resuscitate your husband.' And so they pleaded Kamadeva's case: 'It wasn't Kamadeva's fault,' they said to Shiva. 'We are the ones who told him to disrupt your meditation, because we need your help to fight Tarakasura. Rati is inconsolable. We beg you give her back her beloved and also save us from the asura who is threatening to destroy us.'

'What is done is done,' Shiva said. 'I can't restore a body that is ashes, but Rati will certainly get her husband back. Kamadeva will regain his physical form in Krishna's soon-to-be-born son, Pradyumna. And his spirit I will revive within myself.'

The Great God's anger towards Kamadeva had abated, but the apocalyptic fire that had spewed from his third eye was still raging all around, and the three worlds were on the verge of annihilation. The panicked gods and sages now ran to Brahma for help. Brahma then took the fire of Shiva's fury and, suppressing it, shaped it into a mare. Leading this fiery mare to the seashore, Brahma commanded the Ocean: 'This is the fire of Shiva's fury. I want you to keep her in you and bear her till the time of dissolution. She will subsist by drinking your waters. At the end of this Mahayuga, this Great Age, I will relieve you.'

The ocean accepted Brahma's diktat. No other, except the ocean, could have borne Shiva's fury. That blazing fire in the form of a mare entered the ocean, and there she will remain. At the end of time, Brahma will release the mare, and she will ignite the world.

CREATURES OF THE EARTH

BEHEMOTH THE LAND MONSTER

Behemoth is a huge, hippopotamesque creature who lives in the invisible Dundayin desert, that lies East of Eden. God created only one Behemoth, because he alone can eat up all the grass from a thousand mountains every day; grass is what he feeds on, like an ox. He also needs so much water to quench his thirst that he can drink up all the water of river Jordan. That is why God has created for him the stream of Yubal, which flows from Paradise. Because his appetite and thirst are so voracious, the Behemoth's belly is big and protruding, and Christians fear him like they do the sin of gluttony.

He is also feared for his powerful body. The kernel of his strength is in his loins, and his force is in the core of his belly. His tail is rigid like the cedar, and his sinews are closely knit. His bones are as strong as tubes of brass, and his limbs are like bars of iron. But if one were to go looking for Behemoth, one would find him lounging in the marsh, hidden in the wild lotuses.

Once a year, at the summer solstice, in the month of Tammuz of the Jewish calendar, the Behemoth rears up on his hind legs and roars—the sound is so loud, it is heard from earth to heaven. When the other wild creatures of the world hear his roar, they become terrified, and their bodies resound with the memory of that sound for the rest of the year, making them live in constant fear of the tremendous beast.

The Behemoth is male, to counter the Leviathan's femaleness. At the time of Revelation, the Behemoth and the Leviathan will lock in mortal combat. Then God will slay them both with his mighty sword and serve their meat in a banquet for the righteous.

THE SHE-CAMEL

The She-Camel was a miraculous creature. She was sent by Allah to test the Thamud.

The Thamud tribe lived in Al-Hijr—a region between Madinah and Syria—in the north-west corner of Arabia. Its people were wealthy agriculturalists, who grew corn and fruits and lived in rich houses made of stone. They were arrogant non-believers, enjoying luxury and extravagance, while oppressing the poor, denying them water and pasture, even on free land. So Allah sent them his messenger, Salih, who was one of their own brethren. 'Worship Allah,' Salih advised them. 'You have no other God but Him. Ask forgiveness of Him and turn to Him for repentance.'

But the Thamud were suspicious of Salih and asked him to show them a sign from Allah. Pointing to the remote rock, Al-Katibah, they challenged him to produce a pregnant she-camel from it.

'If Allah shows you this miracle, will you take an oath that you will become believers?' Salih asked.

'Yes,' they said, and Salih began to pray to Allah.

Suddenly, the rock of Al-Katibah shattered, and from it emerged a she-camel; her belly was big, and the calf in it was moving, ready to be born. 'Here is your test,' Salih told the people. 'Allow this she-camel to graze freely in the pastures and let her drink from the water well. So that the water is not depleted, she will drink from the well on one day, and you may drink from it on the next; on the day you abstain, she will provide you milk. 'But,' Salih warned them, 'if you deny Allah's revelation and do her harm, you will suffer grievous punishment.'

After birthing her calf, the she-camel began to roam the land, grazing freely and drinking from the water well one day, giving milk the next. She was so wonderous in her beauty that whenever she passed the other animals in the pasture, they drew away from her in awe.

When they witnessed this miracle, some of the Thamud became believers. However, there were others, like the old, wealthy woman, Umm Ghanem Unayzah, who bore a great enmity towards Salih. There was also another woman, whose name was Saduf bint Al-Muhayya bin Dahr bin Al-Muhayya, and she was from a noble family. She also opposed Salih. Both these women offered a reward to anyone who would kill the camel. Nine prominent men came forward and lured the whole tribe into agreeing to do the deed.

One day the tribe gathered near the water well, and when the camel was leaving it, a man called Mussadi shot an arrow at her and pierced her heel, and another man, Qudar, struck her leg with a sword. The camel fell to the ground, screaming a warning to her calf. Qudar then stabbed her in the neck and killed her.

Seeing its mother fall, the calf climbed onto a rock and screamed in grief three times and then vanished into the stone.

When news of how the camel was hamstrung and slaughtered reached Salih, he rushed to the spot and announced a warning to the tribesmen: 'Enjoy yourself in your homes for three days.'

The nine men who had ordered the camel's slaughter

then decided to make a covert night attack on Salih. They also made a covenant among themselves to lie about the attack so that when Salih's relatives asked, they would all say, 'We know nothing about it.' But, that night, before the attack on Salih could be executed, Allah rained down stones on the heads of those nine men and destroyed them. Now the rest of the Thamud people, who had been party to the She-Camel's slaughter, became afraid of what awaited them after three days, and each of the three days was itself wrought with dread—an equivalent punishment for the three times that the calf had cried. A day after the slaughter, when the Thamud awoke, their faces were pale from fear. The second day was Friday, the day of respite. When they woke up on this day, their faces were red with regret. On the third day, when they arose, their bodies were fragrant with the herb that is used to prepare the dead for burial.

That night, a mighty rumbling came from within the earth and, as the people lay secure in their homes, an earthquake shattered their houses and buried them in the rubble. Allah hid them from the light and removed them from sight, as though they had never existed.

AKOMAN THE EVIL MIND

An evil mind harbours evil purpose because it is invaded by Akoman. Zoroastrians believe Akoman to be the most dreaded of all demons, because he perverts the minds of people and defeats their sense of right and wrong.

This daeva is called Aka Manah in the Gathas, and he was created as sensual desire to seduce Zarathustra. But the Prophet was not seduced. The *Bundahishn* calls him Akoman and says that he, along with his companions, Anashtih (non-peace) and Varun (lust), came into existence to disrupt Ahura Mazda's creation of the world. When Frashokereti, the final battle for the renovation of the universe, occurs all evil will be destroyed, and everything that remains will live in perfect harmony with Ahura Mazda. At that time, Akoman, the daeva of Evil Purpose, will be vanquished by Vohu Manah, the Amesha Spenta of Good Purpose. But, until then, whenever a newborn cries, it will be because Akoman is frightening him with images of Frashokereti.

In the *Shahnameh*, Akoman is in the corporeal form of Akvan—a wild ass, large and powerful, with a yellow hide that has a thick black stripe from mane to tail. Rostam chases him on horseback for three days and three nights, but whenever he gets close enough to shoot an arrow, Akvan conceals himself with magic. Finally, when Rostam lies down to rest, exhausted, Akvan quietly approaches him and, cutting away the earth around him, lifts him up to the sky. 'Do you want to be thrown upon a mountain or be hurled into the sea?' he asks. Rostam prefers the sea, but knowing that the daeva's mind is perverse, he asks to be thrown onto the mountain. Akvan flings him into the sea, and Rostam is able to swim to safety and find his horse, Raksh. Then Rostam confronts Akvan again, and this time, he snares him with his lasso and beheads him.

However, Akoman rarely makes himself visible. It is believed that he is so repugnant that if one were to see him, one's eyes would be blinded.

THE GOLDEN MONGOOSE

The mongoose was a sacrificial animal in Vedic times. At major yajnas, like the Ashvamedha, a sacrifice of lions, tigers, and mongooses was made to Pusan, the god of pathways and journeys, because he guided souls through life and death. While lions and tigers were sacrificed to banish their danger, the mongoose was sacrificed to ward off evil. In Harappa, the mongoose was a protector. Archaeologists have discovered amulets engraved with its image. It is possible that in pre-Vedic times people kept mongooses in granaries for pest control, which may explain their significance as charms to ward off evil.

The mongoose saw the yugas pass, and when it emerged in epical times, it was to condemn large scale and animal sacrifices. After the Great Mahabharata, when Yudhishthira was celebrating his victory and securing his position as monarch of Hastinapur by performing an Ashvamedha horse sacrifice, a blue-eyed mongoose suddenly appeared at the yajna. One side of his body was grey, and the other side was golden. Speaking in a human voice, that was as loud and deep as thunder, he denounced the lavish yajna as unworthy—not even equal to a handful of powdered barley given with a pure and selfless heart. He then recounted the story of a poor Brahmin family that gave their last morsel to him when he was visiting them, disguised as a Brahmin guest. Just the fragrance of that selflessly offered fistful of barley and the touch of ritual water, with which they washed his feet, turned half of his body golden. From that moment on, he began frequenting sacrificial sites and hermitages to, perchance, change the colour of other half of his body. His arrival at Yudhishthira's renowned sacrifice was with the same intent. But it proved futile. 'I am Dharma,' he announced to the honoured kings and Brahmins gathered there. 'And I declare this sacrifice to be worthless. It could not turn even a fraction of my body golden.' Then he left in disgust.

The mongoose is fully golden when it is associated with the gods of wealth. Kubera, the keeper of treasures, is often seen holding a golden mongoose that spits jewels. The wealth-giving Black Jambhala, a manifestation of Buddha Amoghasiddhi, also holds a jewel-spitting newla[6] (mongoose) to bestow prosperous life. But, just as Kubera has a mace to punish those who indulge in the unrightful use of wealth, so does the Jambhala hold a kapala (a skull cup) to indicate that wealth must be used with wisdom.

At some point in time, the mongoose became an enemy of snakes. An Ahir folk tale gives a reason for the acrimony: once, when Shiva was away, Parvati, longing for offspring, ate spinach to become pregnant. She spent seven months yearning for Shiva. Then, pulling out a hair from her head, she turned it into a venomous cobra and sent it to Mahadeva. When the cobra came to Shiva and hissed at him, dripping poison from its fangs, Shiva threw a piece of wood at it to shoo it away. The wood became a mongoose and chased the cobra back to Parvati. Since then, there has been bad blood between mongooses and snakes. And, because the

---

[6]Newla, in Hindi, also means purse.

mongoose is perceived as a protector, the snake became the embodiment of evil.

This is the reason why Kipling's furry, grey mongoose, Rikki-Tikki-Tavi bites off Nag's head to protect little Teddy. And when Nagina comes to avenge her mate, Rikki not only destroys all her eggs, save one, but he also chases her back to her lair and kills her. Thus, the English family's house and garden is safe from snakes because of the mongoose.

The Bodhisattva once tried to resolve this perpetual enmity between the mongoose and the snake. In *Nakula Jataka,* while living as a hermit in the Himalaya, he watches a nakula (mongoose) in an ant heap and a snake in a hollowed tree, quarrelling with each other every day. 'You ought to cease your quarrelling and live together in peace,' he advises the mongoose one day.

'I can't,' the mongoose says.

'Why? What are you afraid of?' the Bodhisattva asks.

'Never despise a former enemy, but always suspect him,' the mongoose replies.

'Fear not,' the Bodhisattva says. 'I have persuaded the snake to do you no harm; distrust him no more.'

Little does the nakula know that it is not the snake that imperils him but the rashness of humans.

The *Panchatantra* tells the story of a Brahmin, Devasharma, and his wife, who takes care of their only son, along with an orphaned mongoose. She showers equal love on both of them and nurses them on her breast. Once, going to fetch water, she tells her husband to watch over the boy and the mongoose. But the Brahmin, too, soon leaves to go and beg for alms. While they are both away, a black cobra slithers into the house. The mongoose, fearing for its brother's life, fights the snake and tears it to pieces. When the woman returns, she sees that the mongoose's fur and mouth are red with blood. Thinking that it has devoured her son, she throws her water-pot at him and kills him.

THE DOG THAT GUARDS THE JUDGEMENT BRIDGE

On the fourth day after death, the soul of a Parsi goes to the Chinavat Bridge of Judgement. Here it is met by Daena, the divinity of Revelation. If the person has led a righteous life, Daena appears as a beautiful maiden, but if this person has lived a life of lies, she is an ugly crone. Daena is accompanied by a yellow dog that has a dark patch around each eye, making it look four-eyed. Sometimes, the dog is white with yellow ears. This dog is the earthly representative of Sraosha Yazata, the divinity of conscience. It is he who directs the soul to the path of just rewards—toward demons who drag it to hell, or towards the vision of heaven.

When a person dies, a piece of bread is placed on the body three times; these are the portions of the dog, and he will come to get them three times. While living, if a person keeps three morsels of food aside from every meal to give to the dog, he can be saved from the torments of hell.

It is the dog who knows whether a person who is presumed to be dead is really dead or not. When this dog is brought to the dead body, the druj-e nashush—microbes of decomposition—that have become foul flies, scatter and flee to the regions of the north. This is because the dog's eyes emit such strong magnetic currents that they chase away the noxious microbes. This is the ritual of Sagdid—the glance of the dog. His visitation provides protection to the departing soul.

The Avesta says that the vohunazga dogs, who are stray and belong to no one, follow the corpse bearers to the place of exposure, and it is they who devour the corpse, because the corpse demon cannot harm them.[7]

To kill a vohunazga dog is to incur perdition.

---

[7]In later traditions, the corpses were left to be devoured by vultures.

REEM A MOUNTAIN WITH HORNS

The reem is a mountainous, horned creature. Within a day of its birth, it grows as large as Israel's Mount Tabor.

There are only two reems in existence at any given time—a male and a female, and they live separately, a world apart; one lives in the east and one in the west. They come together every seventy years to mate and procreate, and immediately after she conceives, the female bites the male, and he dies. The pregnant female reem gestates for twelve years, but by the eleventh year, she becomes so big that she is unable to move. All she can do is roll from side to side and, as she does this, she drools profusely. This spittle keeps the land around her abundantly green with vegetation, and that is how she sustains herself for the twelfth year. When her time comes, her belly bursts, and a pair of reems fall out, while she herself expires. Soon after being birthed, the new male and female reems begin drifting to opposite ends of world, growing to their full size within a day. And the cycle repeats.

If reems lived together, or copulated more often, or if the parents didn't die soon after birthing a new pair, the world would not be able to sustain the population of these mountain-sized creatures.

A traveller once saw a one-day old reem. He described its height as four parasangs,[8] and the length of just its head,

---

[8]Parasang was a measure of distance in ancient Persia. One parasang is about six kilometres.

a parasang-and-a-half. He also said that it had horns that measure one hundred ells[9].

Once, when King David was a young shepherd, he came upon a sleeping reem. Thinking it was a mountain, he climbed up its side. When the reem suddenly moved, David lost his footing and grabbed on to one of its horns. The creature stood up, and David found himself rising, almost up to heaven. Seeing him hanging precariously from the reem's horn, God sent down a lion. As soon as the reem saw the lion, it became afraid and knelt before it, bringing David closer to the earth. He desperately wanted to jump down and flee, but he, too, was terrified of the ferocious lion. Understanding his dilemma, God then sent down a gazelle. When the lion leapt at the gazelle, David let go off the reem's horn and, landing on his feet, ran away as fast as he could. That is why the Bible says about dilemmas: 'Rescue me from the mouth of the lion; save me from the horns of the reem' (Psalm 22:21).

---

[9]Cubits.

TEKHUMIAVI A DREAMSCAPE

The Angamis, one of the tribes of Nagaland, speak in hushed tones about the tekhumiavi—a man whose soul has transferred into a tiger's body, while his human body is still alive and intact. This state can last one night or longer, and while it lasts, it is as though the man is in a dream, but the dreamscape is real. In the tiger's body, he behaves like a tiger; he ranges through vast forests, he roars, he hunts, and he preys, tearing the meat with his carnassials. As his tiger body engages in these tiger activities, his human body, lying in deep sleep, convulses. And if the tiger gets wounded, the human body displays the bruises. When the man's soul returns to his body, his joints and muscles swell up from the strain that he has put on them in tiger pursuits. He also retains full memory of his tiger sojourn.

A tekhumiavi is not easily detectable. The only sign that a tiger has been possessed by a soul traveller is in his pugmarks; they show an imprint of five claws, instead of four.

Most Naga tribes believe that the tiger and man are meant to coexist; they have a common ancestry. According to a commonly known Naga folk tale, the first tiger and the first man were brothers; sons of the same mother, separated only because of their differing behaviours. That is why it is taboo for men to kill tigers, for it would be tantamount to killing a brother. Because the two share a bloodline, the ability of transference from one body to another is a continuum. This faculty is mostly inherited, passing from father to son, sometimes skipping a generation. But it can also be acquired through a ritual, which involves a tekhumiavi sharing a dish of ginger and chicken with an aspirant.

JAMBAVANA THE MONKEY BEAR

Jambavana was born six months before the earth was created. At first there was nothingness. From it emerged the sound of Om. Then a lotus formed in the primordial waters. And in the lotus, a hairy animal came into existence. This was Jambavana, and as soon as he was born, he became immersed in tapas, practising severe austerities. Then Adi Shakti emerged from the lotus. She had five faces, ten hands, and three eyes; the third eye in her forehead was capable of burning whatever it looked upon. She had stars on her tongue, mantras in her mouth, and a chintamani, wish-granting jewel, in her navel. She birthed three eggs, from which were born Brahma, Vishnu, and Shiva. Jambavana advised these gods to seize Adi Shakti's third eye, and with the fire of that eye, they burnt her to ashes. From her own ashes, Adi Shakti was resurrected, and the three gods divided her into five parts: The first three were Sarasvati, Lakshmi, and Parvati, and they were created to be the wives of the three gods. The fourth part yielded two other women who were espoused to Jambavana. From the fifth part, Kali came into being.

To be married to the three chief gods, the would-be brides, Sarasvati, Lakshmi, and Parvati needed jewellery, which required the creation of precious metals and stones. Vishwabrahma and other craftsmen were able to forge the metals and gems, but they did not a have the means to smelt them. For that bellows were required. Jambavana promised to provide leather bellows, but there was no material with which to construct them, because cows had not yet come into existence. Jambavana then created a son, Yugamunindrudu, from the right side of his own stomach and killed him so that his skin and bones could be used for the purpose. Thus, with bellows made of human skin, metals were smelted and jewellery was made for the brides of the gods, and, finally, their marriage was celebrated. After that the rest of the universe was created.

This is a tale that the Madiga tribes of Telangana perform in their Chindu dance dramas. This origin tale establishes the link between the divine and the leatherworks livelihood that the Madigas of Andhra Pradesh, Karnataka, and Telangana practise. And, since Jambavana provided them their trade, they worship him and his wives as ancestors.

Another Chindu dance drama, Yakshagana, depicts the story of how Jambavana also provided the Madigas the knowledge of dance and its accoutrements: once, in a battle between devas and asuras, the devas enlisted Kali's help to destroy the asura, Raktabija, who had a boon that each drop of his blood that fell on the ground would become one thousand more Raktabijas. Battling the asura, Kali drank up his blood before any of it could spill on the ground. However, the drinking of blood fuelled Kali's rage, and after demolishing Raktabija, she turned on the gods. Terrified of Kali's uncontrolled wrath, the gods pleaded Jambavana for help. To accomplish this great and difficult task, Jambavana required the gods' assistance, and they presented him with thirty badges of honour, which included the distinctive Madiga drum (dappu) created by Vishnu; a tiger skin that belonged to Shiva; and ankle bells (gajjelu) strung together by Virabhadra. Dancing with these on, Jambavana pacified the fury of Kali and then returned to his home in Jambalagiri.

The Puranas say that Jambavana was Kapishreshtha, the foremost among monkeys. He was Riksharaj, king of the Rikshas, who, in earlier literatures, were species of Vanaras (monkeys). In Valmiki's Ramayana, Jambavana is a monkey, but, by the time Tulsidas's *Ramcharitamanasa* was composed, he became a bear.

In most versions of the Ramayana, Jambavana is an old and wise bear, living in the Vanara kingdom of Kishkindha. He makes an appearance when the Vanaras view with trepidation the vast and turbulent ocean they need to cross to get to Lanka and rescue Sita. It is Jambavana who reminds Hanuman of his divine lineage and his ability to leap and fly, and, realizing this, Hanuman goes to Lanka. Then again, in the war against Ravana, when Rama, Lakshmana, and the whole monkey army are rendered unconscious by the Brahma missile that Ravana's son, Indrajita, shoots, it is Jambavana who knows how to cure them. Despite being pierced with ten arrows himself, he instructs Hanuman to go to Himalaya, find the flaming mountain between the peaks of Rishaba and Kailasha, and gather from it the four medicinal herbs that will revive Rama's army.

Jambavana plays a role in Krishna's life as well. The Bhagavata Purana narrates a tale about how Krishna was once accused by the Yadava king, Satrajita, of killing his brother, Prasena, and of stealing the lustrous Syamantaka jewel from him. Prasena had, in fact, been killed by a lion, who had leapt on him to snatch the sun-bright jewel necklace. At that time, Jambavana, a bear chief, lived in a dark cave in the forest, and he had taken the jewel from the lion to give to his son as a toy. Searching for the jewel, Krishna traced it to Jambavana's cave and attacked him. They battled for twenty-eight days, until a badly wounded Jambavana realized that the reason he could not defeat the intruder was because he was no other than Rama himself. Falling at his feet, he begged Krishna for forgiveness and offered him his daughter, Jambavanti, along with the precious Syamantaka jewel. Raising Jambavana by the shoulders, Krishna removed his pain with just a touch. Then he blessed him with immortality.

UCHCHAIHSHRAVAS
THE COSMIC HORSE

Uchchaihshravas is a white, winged horse with seven heads. He was born from the cosmic ocean. When devas and asuras churned the ocean to obtain amrita, the elixir of immortality, the ocean became the amniotic fluid for many beings; among them, Uchchaihshravas. Emerging from the waters, he soared upwards, his wings fashioned from the sun, his body made for flight, his spirit swift as the wind in motion. Indra, the king of gods, claimed him and made him his vahana, his mount.

Once Rishi Kashyapa's two wives, Kadru, the mother of snakes, and Vinata, the mother of the birds, Garuda and Aruni, laid a wager about Uchchaihshravas's colour. Vinata said he was white, and Kadru said he was black. To win the wager, Kadru had her thousand snake sons braid themselves in the tail of the divine horse. Thus, when the two sisters looked upon the horse at dawn, they saw his tail was black, and Vinata, losing the bet, became Kadru's slave for five hundred years. Hence, through the deception of a capricious wager, Uchchaihshravas became the causal divide between the sky-rangers and those who range on the earth and in the worlds below. However, for this very reason Uchchaihshravas is also bound to the three worlds and is a bridge between them. Three of his bonds are in heaven, three on earth, and three within the ocean.

When the mythical King Prithu levelled out Prithvi to

make the earth habitable, he bestowed sovereignty on certain beings and allotted them responsibility of specific segments of creation. At that time, Uchchaihshravas was made king of horses.

The Yajur Veda says that on earth, a sacrificer who sacrifices the sovereign steed in the Ashvamedha yajna gains sovereignty. The Rig Veda declares this divine steed as the cosmic male archetype; his prolific seed is soma. Therefore, during the Ashvamedha yajna, when the queen lay in ritual copulation with the dead steed, she was, in fact, copulating with the cosmic male sovereign to invigorate his energy and bring fertility to the land. In the Ashvamedha, the universe itself is conceived as a horse.

In the Bhagavad Gita, Krishna tells Arjuna, 'Of horses, know me as Uchchaihshravas' (10:27).

KUYUTHA THE COSMIC BULL

Kuyutha is a cosmic bull. He has four thousand eyes, or perhaps, forty thousand; whatever the count, his ears, noses, and tongues also number the same, and between each set of eyes is a distance equal to a journey of five hundred years. He takes a breath only twice a day; when he exhales the seas flow, and when he inhales the waters ebb.

Allah has created seven firmaments. The seventh heaven is Jannat. The earth, too, has seven layers; humans dwell in the topmost. According to Islamic cosmography, when Allah first erected this universe, it was unstable, so Allah created an immense angel and told him to hold the heavens and earths on his shoulders. Gripping the east and west ends with his two hands, the angel held the universe steady, but his feet were unsupported. Hence, Allah created a rock made of ruby that had seven thousand perforations, each one issuing a great sea, and he placed this rock under the feet of the angel. However, the rock itself was unsteady. Thus, it was that Allah created the immense bull, Kuyutha. Placing the bull under the ruby rock, he told him to hold it up between his hump and horns. But now there was no support for the bull and despite his own size, he tottered under the combined weight of the universe, the angel, and the ruby rock from which seven thousand seas flowed. Therefore, Allah created a fish so big and with such flashing eyes that no one could look upon it. He placed the fish below the bull, and to support the fish, he spread water beneath it, and, underneath the water, he spread darkness. Under the darkness....

Mankind's knowledge is too limited to understand what is under the darkness.

NANDI THE DHARMA BULL

Nandi is Shiva in the form of a humped white bull. The bull is dharma.

The Linga Purana tells the story of Nandi's birth: once a pious sage, Shilada, desiring a son, propitiated Shiva by doing a thousand years of penance. When his body became a mere skeleton, and his skin began crawling with worms, Shiva came to him and asked him what he desired. 'I wish for a son who is not born from a womb, and who will live without fear of death—a son who is equal to you.'

Shiva granted his boon. 'I will become your son,' he said. 'I will not be born in a womb, and I will be deathless. My name will be Nandi. I am father of all the worlds, and now you will be my father.'

Nandi was born from Shilada's yajna fire. He had three eyes, four arms, and the lustre of the gods Yama, Surya, and Agni. His hair was matted, and he wore a coronet, like a new moon. He even held a trident in his hand. In other words, he was an exact replica of Shiva.

Shilada received his son like a treasure. However, as soon as he brought him home, his divine attributes fell off, and he became an ordinary boy. Shilada bemoaned this loss, but he was grateful that, at least, he had a son. Performing his natal ceremonies, he began educating him in the Vedic way.

Once, when the boy was seven, the gods Mitra and Varuna came to Shilada's hermitage. Noticing certain signs on the boy, they pronounced that his life would be short.

When Shilada heard this devastating prediction, he fainted, and distressed by his father's sorrow, the boy took a vow that he would alter his ordained lifespan by doing penance to Shiva. Hence, he began the very arduous Rudra Japa to appease Shiva's Rudra form and remove the malefic effect of his birth planets. Finally, Shiva manifested before the boy and made these pronouncements: 'You are equal to me and will always be. You will experience neither death nor old age. You will be the leader of my ganas; my favourite of all the ganas. You will gain strength from me and will always be at my side.' And, just before he disappeared, Shiva threw his own necklace of lotuses around the boy's head. As soon as that garland touched him, he became three-eyed and ten-armed, like a second Shiva. Then, taking Ganga water in his cupped palm from the stream that was flowing from his locks, Shiva sprinkled it on the boy and said, 'Be Nandin (happy)!'

In the Shiva Purana, Nandi himself narrates the story of another bull form that Shiva assumed during the Samudra Manthan: when the devas and danavas were churning the ocean to gain amrita, and Dhanvantri, the celestial healer, emerged from the water, holding the amrita vessel, many droplets of the elixir fell in a spray around him. These crores of droplets turned into frolicking maidens, as beautiful as a full moon in an autumn sky. The danavas, who were deprived of the amrita by the gods, grabbed these women and took them to their homes in Patala, challenging the gods to rescue them, if they could.

When the gods, headed by Vishnu, broke into the netherworld to liberate the women, Vishnu saw that they had all become intoxicated with desire. Hence, instead of liberating them, he embraced them and begot many sons from them. These sons grew up strong, valorous, and passionate, and they began harassing everyone in heaven and earth. To restrain these sons full of passion, Brahma and the other gods approached Shiva in Kailasha and asked for his help. Shiva then took the form of Rishabha, the bull, who was as tall as a mountain, and attacked Vishnu's sons, kicking them with his hooves and ripping their flesh with his horns. Seeing his sons destroyed, Vishnu fought with Rishabha, but couldn't withstand his power. With a final bellow that shook the three worlds, Rishabha, the bull, leapt on Vishnu and defeated him.

The bull is Shiva's theriomorphic form. While Rishabha represents the control of the rampant passion, Nandi represents sexual energy. By riding Nandi, Shiva shows that although he is in constant love-play with Parvati, his desire is under his control.

BUDDHA THE WHITE ELEPHANT

For seven days before the full moon, Queen Maya participated in the festivities of the midsummer festival. On the seventh day, she rose early and bathed in water perfumed with roses and sandalwood. After distributing wealth among the destitute and holy, she returned to her rooms and, dressing in queenly finery, lay down on her royal couch to rest. Soon, she fell asleep and, in her sleep, she had a dream: the guardian gods of heaven were lifting her couch and taking it to a crimson plain in the Himalaya. There they placed the couch under a great sala tree. Then the queens of the gods took Queen Maya to Lake Anottota and bathed her in it. Adorning her with heavenly flowers, they brought her to a golden mansion on Silver Hill and lay her on a divine couch, turning her head to the east. Then, the Bodhisattva, in the form of a pure white elephant, holding a white lotus with his silver trunk, approached the golden mansion from the north, and circumambulating Queen Maya three times, struck her side and entered her womb.

When Maya woke up, she shared her dream with her husband, King Sudodhana. The king summoned sixty-four eminent Brahmins and, honouring them with wealth and milk and honey, requested them to interpret the queen's dream.

'You will have a son,' the Brahmins told the king. 'If he adopts a householder's life, he will become a king, a universal monarch. But if he leaves his home and adopts a religious life, he will become a Buddha, full of compassion, who will remove veils of ignorance and sin from the world.'

◆

Once, the Bodhisattva was born as a chaddanta elephant of six tusks. Chaddanta was pure white, and his face and paws were bright red. He lived near a lake in the golden cave of Kanchanaguha with his two queens, Mahasubhadda and Chullasubhadda. One day, the younger queen suffered some inadvertent humiliation at the hands of the elder queen, but Chaddanta sided with the elder. The younger queen was peeved, and she carried this grudge with her into the next life. In her new birth, she married the king of Varanasi and persuaded him to send a hunter to find Chaddanta in Kanchanaguha and cut off his tusks. The hunter, Sanuttara, searched for Chaddanta's cave for seven years, seven months, and seven days, and when he finally found it, he trapped the elephant and shot him with a poisoned arrow. The wounded Chaddanta turned to charge at him, but when he saw that the man was dressed in a saffron robe, he stopped. Then, knowing what the hunter wanted, he sawed off his own tusks and handed them to him. When Sanuttara brought the six trunks back to the queen, she died of shock.

Another time the Bodhisattva was born in a Himalayan forest as Silava, a white elephant. His body was like silver, his eyes were like diamond balls, his mouth was red, like scarlet velvet, his trunk was silver, flecked with red gold, and his four paws looked like polished lac. One day, while he was walking in the forest, he met a man who had lost his way and was in great distress. Filled with compassion, Silava raised the man onto his back and took him to the path that led to Varanasi. But this was a greedy man. As soon as he arrived in Varanasi, he went to the market and enquired about the price of ivory. Then he went to Silava and asked him for his tusks. The elephant agreed to have half his tusks sawed off. The greedy man sold the half tusks, spent the money, and then returned to Silava for more. Silava let him saw off the remainder of the tusks, as well. But the man came back again; this time to take the stumps. Climbing onto Silava's head, which was like Mount Kailasha, he wrenched the stumps out from the flesh and left Silava bleeding to death.

After selling the stumps of ivory, as this man was returning home, a great big flaming chasm opened in his path and swallowed him. He ended up in the bowels of the earth, suffering the torments of hell.

MAHISA THE MAJESTIC

Mahisa, the buffalo, is famous for his death. He was the reason the gods invoked Goddess Durga, and his salvation was her prime purpose.

The buffalo may have been a deity in the pre-Aryan era. The well-known Pashupati seal from the Indus Valley Civilization that early scholars explained as proto-Shiva wearing a horned headdress may actually be an image of proto-Mahisa, a composite man–buffalo with the curved horns of a wild buffalo. Hence, some scholars have surmised that Mahisa of the Durga myth may be a mythicized form of a buffalo cult of Harappa.

The Devi Mahatmya tells this myth: Mahisa was born to avenge the daityas. When, in a battle with the devas, the daityas were utterly destroyed, Diti, the mother of the daityas, distraught with grief, asked her daughter to bear a powerful son through asceticism, who would be able to destroy the gods. The daughter then took the form of a she-buffalo and went to the forest, where she practised rigorous asceticism: building four fires around her, she sat down under the fiery sun and bore the extreme heat for hundreds of years. Finally, she received a boon from Shiva that she would give birth to a majestic son whose name would be Mahisa. He would have a man's body and buffalo's head, and he would have the ability to take any form at will. Being invincible, no god would be able to destroy him, and he would fight the devas and topple Indra.

Even as he was born, Mahisa grew to enormous size, his energy swelling like the ocean during a lunar tide. Immediately after his birth, he went to heaven and wrecked Indra's garden, Nandanavana. Then, he demolished the rest of heaven and began hurling the devas to the earth. He also began ravaging the earth by uprooting mountains with the tips of his horns, crushing minerals under his hooves, and striking the ocean with his head, demanding that it give up all its gems. Terrified of him and acknowledging the powerlessness of their masculine strength, the gods begged Goddess Gauri for help.

Gauri agreed to assist the devas, and, changing herself into a lovely maiden called Durga, she went to Arunachala Mountain, where Mahisa was destroying the flora and fauna. When Mahisa heard about the maiden and her unsurpassable beauty, he sent his generals to proposition her on his behalf. At Durga's refusal, Mahisa grew enraged and, making himself as large as Mount Meru, went to her himself, bringing with him his whole daitya army. Seeing Durga surrounded by the daityas, each of the gods bestowed upon her his own strongest weapon to equip her for battle. Armed with these divine weapons, Durga became more powerful than any of the gods, and, mounting her fiery-maned, sinewy lion, Dawon, who was given to her by Himavata, the lord of mountains, she faced Mahisa, challenging him to fight her.

Mahisa pounded the earth with his massive hooves and, digging his horns into the roots of mountains, tossed them up like pebbles. With his powerful tail, he lashed the waters of the ocean until they overflowed and flooded the earth. The Goddess hurled her noose at his buffalo head, but he left his buffalo form and became a lion. Durga's own lion pounced on him in an attempt to tear open his chest; but instantly, Mahisa became a man, wielding a deadly sword and protecting himself with a shield of hide. When the Goddess assailed him with arrows, he became an elephant and grabbed her lion with his trunk. She cut off his trunk, but he became a buffalo again and shook himself so violently, the three worlds trembled.

Flustered by his rapidly shifting shape and immense strength, the Goddess fortified herself by gulping down cups of wine laced with soma. Then, calling all her shaktis to permeate her, she turned to face him again, her eyes raging red with wrath. Mahisa, too, was intoxicated—not with wine, but his own strength. Lifting mountains on his horns, he hurled them at Durga, but she shattered them all with her arrows. Then, with a maniacal laugh, she leapt on the daitya and, mounting on his shoulders, kicked him in the neck with her foot. Weighed down by the Goddess and all the shaktis that she had summoned within her, Mahisa staggered. Taking advantage of his weakened state, Durga pierced him with her trident. An ocean of blood poured out of Mahisa's body, and his spirit emerged from his mouth. Right at that opportune moment, Durga cut off his head and flung it on the ground. Then, trampling on Mahisa's severed head, the Goddess danced in victory.

Mahisa attained salvation, because he was destroyed by the Goddess's divine weapons, which struck like an epiphany of knowledge. He also became a symbol of truth and righteousness by virtue of bearing her footprint on his neck. That is why, when Durga killed him, she announced to the world: 'Whoever worships me, must also worship Mahisa.'

AIRAVATA THE KING OF ELEPHANTS

White as the cosmic ocean of milk, endowed with seven trunks and four tusks, the resplendent divine king of elephants is Airavata. Created from a shell of the egg from which Garuda was born, he is, in essence, the golden bird's sibling. After Garuda hatched, Brahma took one half of his eggshell in his right hand and recited seven shlokas over it. Thus, Airavata, the first elephant, came into existence, and, right after, seven other male divine elephants were born. To provide them with mates, Brahma then blew on the eggshell in his left hand and created eight she-elephants. Together, these eight pairs became the guardians of the four quarters. Airavata and his wife guard the east; that is why Airavata is also called Arka Sodara, the brother of the sun.

Airavata's father was Rishi Kashyapa, the sage whose allegory is Kurma, the cosmic tortoise, and his mother is River Irawati. Hence, he is called Airavata, and that is also why he is always associated with water. He is Abhra-matang, the elephant of the clouds, and his wife is Abhramu, the one who knits the clouds together. There was a time, an earlier time, a time even before Airavata was born, when elephants had wings, and they roamed the sky like clouds. Once, wandering in the sky like vagabonds, a herd of elephants alighted on a tree in the northern Himalaya. Under that tree, Rishi Dirghatapa was teaching his disciples. The tree branch on which the elephants landed was unable to bear their weight, and it came crashing down on Dirghatapa's students.

Enraged, the rishi cursed the flying elephants that they would lose their wings so that they would never again range in the sky and alight on trees. Hence, the elephants lost their ability to fly, but their connection to rainclouds remained in cosmic memory, making them a symbol of fertility. That is why Gajalakshmi, the goddess of fertility and abundance, is flanked by elephants with raised trunks, lustrating her.

Even Ganga, the river of deliverance, owes her presence on earth to Airavata. When Raja Bhagiratha sought to bring Ganga from heaven to earth to liberate his ancestors' souls, it was Airavata who smashed the summit of Ushinara at Kankhal in Haridwara to create a suitable spot where the holy river could safely descend. Since then, people have been immersing the ashes of their dead at Kankhal ghat.

Another source of Airavata's origin is the cosmic ocean. During the great Samudra Manthan, when devas and danavas churned the ocean, with Naag Vasuki as churning rope and Mount Mandar as churning stick, many wonderous divine beings arose from the waters: the moon with its thousand rays; Lakshmi, seated on a lotus; Devi Shura, the goddess of intoxication; the fleet as mind, divine horse, Uchchaihshravas; Kaustubha, the gem that adorns Narayana's breast; the parijata tree of never withering flowers; and the cow, Surabhi, the bestower of plenty. Then, the divine healer, Dhanvantri, emerged, holding a vessel filled with amrita; and, following him came Airavata—pure, white, powerful, seven-trunked. Indra the king of gods claimed him as his mount.

Once Indra, riding on Airavata, met Rishi Durvasa, who was in an impassioned state. The rishi gave Indra a garland of flowers, but the arrogant king of gods, not realizing that this was Goddess Shri's garland of never-withering flowers, tossed it away. It landed on Airavata's head, and the elephant, irritated by the buzzing bees in the flowers, threw it to the ground and trampled on it. Seeing the Goddess's garland treated with such disregard, Rishi Durvasa, who is known for his sudden fits of wrath, cursed Indra that he and his legion of devas would be abandoned by Shri. Thus, when Shri, who is prosperity, sovereignty, and the very lustre of gods, left the devas, they lost their godliness. This is the reason why the gods churned the Great Ocean; they needed to acquire amrita to become resplendent again.

In the circularity of myth, Airavata became the cause for the cause, and in the process, he himself was found.

THE HOLY COW
PRITHVI SURABHI DHARMA

There was a mighty king, Vena, born from Punitha, the daughter of Mrityu (Death). Being Death's grandson, Vena was cruel, unfeeling, and arrogant. 'I am king. I am your supreme lord; not Vishnu,' he would say to the Brahmins in his kingdom. 'Obey only me; worship only me; sacrifice only to me.'

One day, outraged at his wicked commands, the sages fell upon Vena and beat him with consecrated blades of grass, till he was dead. But now the kingdom was without a king, and it became an easy conquest for neighbouring rulers. To protect the kingdom, the sages then sought to produce an heir from the slain Vena. They rubbed his thigh until a being emerged from it. He was charred black and dwarfish, like Vena's depravity, and with him the king's wickedness was expelled. Then the rishis rubbed Vena's right arm, and the being which emerged was handsome and resplendent, like Agni; he also had the auspicious mark of Vishnu's chakra in his hand. They named him Prithu, and he became a chakravarti king, his sovereignty extending over the whole earth. Prithu began to rule with virtue and justice; however, in the time that the kingdom had been without a king, Earth had forsaken the land and people were inflicted with a terrible famine.

Angered by Earth's disregard for human suffering, Prithu took up his divine arrows and the Ajagava bow, that Shiva had bestowed on him, and sought Earth to punish her. She took the form of a cow and fled, but he pursued her. Finally, unable to escape Prithu, the Earth Cow faced him, trembling in fear. 'Do you not know the sin of killing a female?' she asked.

'When the destruction of one serves the happiness of many, that killing is a virtue not a sin,' Prithu replied.

'But by killing me you will take way the very means by which your people live,' she said.

'I will support my people with the fruits of my own merit,' he replied.

Realizing that Prithu's intent was to erase her very existence, Earth conceded. 'Give me a suitable calf,' she said. 'From the milk of my udders, I will milk your whole land, and it will become fertile. But you must make the land level so that my milk can flow unimpeded.'

Prithu tore down mountains and levelled the land. He created boundaries for villages and towns, pastures for agriculture, and highways for merchants. Then he requested Swayambhu Manu, mankind's first progenitor, to become Earth's calf. Thus, the Earth Cow was milked, and the earth became fertile for all humanity. From then on, the Earth Cow has been considered Prithu's daughter and is called Prithvi—she who gives to each class of being the milk that it desires.

◆

The all-giving cow is also Surabhi—sweet-smelling. Once, Krishna and Radha were sporting in Vrindavan, and Krishna felt a keen desire to drink milk. He then created Surabhi from his left side and milked her, collecting the milk in an earthenware jar. While Krishna was milking Surabhi, some drops of milk spilled on the ground. These became a vast expanse, called Kshirasagara, the cosmic ocean of milk. After drinking the milk, Krishna felt satiated, and his satisfaction spread to all humanity. Then, from Surabhi's every pore, one lakh koti (crore) Kamadhenu, desire-fulfilling cows were born, and Krishna gave these away to the cowherds. From these Kamadhenu, more were born, and soon the world was filled with cows and milk, and prosperity spread everywhere.

◆

Another aspect of the sacred cow is cosmic dharma. In Vedic times, when Indra killed Vrta, the great serpent dragon that was holding the primordial waters captive, the water gushed out like lowing cows. These cows were pregnant, and they birthed the sun. Then the earth and sky were set in place. This is how Rta, cosmic law, was established, assigning roles for devas, asuras, and mankind, so that creation could be sustained. Thus, the lowing cow is the microcosm of the universe. When she stands with her four hooves firmly planted, she encompasses all four directions. She is complete, she is self-contained, and she is perfection. She is dharma in its full agency. With the passing of each yuga—Krita Yuga, Treta Yuga, Dvapara Yuga, and Kali Yuga—dharma degenerates, and the dharma cow lifts one of her hooves. In the present Kali Yuga, dharma is so diminished that she is tottering on the tip of just one hoof, and when no dharma remains in the world, she will lift that, as well. Then the current cycle of Great Time will stop, and everything will end, annihilating all in the final dissolution. When the universe is renewed and cosmic order is re-established, the dharma cow will once again stand balanced on all four hooves. Then the cycle will resume, and the process will begin anew.

OTHER CREATURES OF AIR, WATER & LAND
WORMS, INSECTS, REPTILES & DRAGONS

AZHI DAHAKA THE CORRUPTER OF THE ORDER

Azhi Dahaka is a monstrous cosmic dragon with three mouths, six eyes, and three heads, one of which is human. He is created from the lies of Angra Mainyu, the destructive spirit, to corrupt Asha, the order of the world, and to thwart the good counsel of Ahura Mazda, who is the creator and chief deity of Zoroastrianism. The Avesta says Azhi Dahaka lives in the inaccessible fortress of Kvirinta in the land of Bawri[10].

Dahaka, as his name suggests, has ten sins. He also has a thousand senses and is invincible. He is cunning and strong, and he possesses enough evil to destroy the corporeal world. He controls diseases and storms and, when he is cut, he bleeds scorpions and snakes and other poisonous creatures.

Once, Dahaka sacrificed a hundred male horses, a thousand oxen, and ten thousand lambs to Anahita, the divinity of waters, and Vayu, the divinity of storm-wind and asked for a boon: 'I want to make the seven continents empty of men. Grant me this.' But Anahita and Vayu refused.

Then the brave Thraetaona, of the glorious Athwya clan, offered a sacrifice of a hundred male horses, a thousand oxen, and ten thousand lambs to Anahita and said: 'Grant me this boon so that I may destroy the three-headed, six-eyed Azhi Dahaka, who has a thousand senses and whose lies destroy

---

[10]Babylon.

the good principle of the world.'

'Granted!' Anahita said to him, and Thraetaona went to battle with Dahaka. Defeating him, he chained the dragon and threw him in a cave in the mythical mountain, Damavand.

The Avestan Thraetaona is Fereydun in Ferdowsi's *Shahnameh*. He is the valorous descendent of Jamshid of the Pishdadian dynasty that was formed by Keymars, the first human. In the *Shahnameh*, Azhi Dahaka is called Zahhak, and he is the son of the Arab king, Merdas. Zahhak murdered his father, claimed the throne, and started oppressing the people. Eblis, whose other name is Ahriman, was pleased with his wicked ways. He came to Zahhak disguised as a cook and declared that he could make such succulent dishes from the flesh of animals and birds that they would surpass anything that he had ever tasted. Zahhak employed him and was so bewitched by his dishes he promised him a reward.

'The only reward I want is to kiss you on both your shoulders,' Eblis replied.

When Zahhak agreed, Eblis placed a kiss on Zahhak's left shoulder, followed by another on the right. Then he disappeared. Suddenly, two black serpents sprouted on Zahhak's shoulders, hissing and flashing their fangs. The king tried to rid himself of the snakes, but every time he sliced them off with his sword, they grew back. Even Zahhak's physicians did not know how to cure the king. Then Eblis came to him again, this time disguised as a physician, and told him that the only way he could stop the snakes from devouring him was to keep them fed with human brains. Hence, Zahhak ordered to have two men killed each day, and he fed their brains to the serpents on his shoulders.

At this time the Persian king of the world was Jamshid.

Zahhak dethroned Jamshid and had him sawn into two. Then, placing the turquoise crown on his own head, he ruled Persia for a thousand years with evil ways. One night he dreamt that the son of the slain warrior, Abetin, was putting him in chains. This boy, Fereydun, was not yet born, and his mother was hiding in the Alburz mountains in India to keep her unborn son safe from the evil designs of Zahhak. Soon after Zahhak saw Fereydun in his dream, his mother birthed him.

When Fereydun became a young man, he gathered an army and mounted an attack on Zahhak. Smashing his skull with his ox-headed mace, he rendered him unconscious, but he did not kill him. He had been warned by the angel Sorush that if Zahhak was killed, his dead body would produce so much evil it would destroy the world. Hence, Fereydun bound Zahhak in chains and kept him below the high volcanic mount of Damavand, and that is where he remains until the end of time.

Pahlavi sources prophesy that the only one capable of killing Dahaka is Kirasap, the last Pishdadian shah, because Kirasap's body is being protected by the fravashi (spirit) of 99,999 righteous people. At the end of the world, Dahaka will break his bonds and ravage the world, and, at that time, Kirasap will be resurrected to destroy him.

THE SERPENT IN
THE GARDEN OF EDEN

The serpent was craftier than any beast that the Lord had made. It also had the ability to speak, and, approaching Eve in the Garden of Eden, he said to her, 'Is it true that God has forbidden you to eat from any tree in the garden?'

Eve answered, 'We may eat the fruit of any tree in the garden except for the tree in the middle. God has forbidden us to eat from it, or even to touch its fruit. If we do this, we will die.'

'Of course, you will not die,' the serpent said. 'God knows that as soon as you eat its fruit, your eyes will open, and you will be like the gods, knowing good and evil. That is why he has forbidden you to eat it.'

Eve looked at the fruit, and, tempted by it, she ate some of it. She also shared it with her husband, Adam. As soon as Adam and Eve ate the fruit, they became aware that they were naked, and they were ashamed. To hide their nakedness, they stitched together fig leaves and made loincloths.

◆

The serpent, Nachash, was cognizance, because the forbidden tree was, after all, the Tree of Knowledge. He was also temptation; or, perhaps, sexual desire. He tempted Eve, because Eve, whose name means 'source of life', was herself full of life's desires. That is why when some High

Renaissance artists, like Mariotto Albertinelli, painted the Garden of Eden, they gave the serpent a face that looked like Eve's.

The temptation of Eve may, indeed, have been the serpent's trickery, because he was a powerful trickster—a great red dragon with seven heads and ten horns, with seven diadems on his heads and a tail that swept down a third of the stars from the sky and flung them on earth. In the past, he himself had been thrown down to earth by Archangel Michael and his angels in the heavenly war. His name used to be Lucifer, the 'light bringer', but when he rebelled against God, he became Satan, or the Devil, and he began to rule over the kingdom of darkness. Ever since he and his legion of fallen angels were cast to the earth, he has been trying to seduce Christians with evil, and he will continue to do so till the Day of Judgement, when God will finally destroy him.

◆

Adam and Eve fell for the serpent's temptation. Their act of disobedience to God and their subsequent shame was the Fall of Man. Having eaten the forbidden fruit and discovered their naked selves, they hid from God in the Garden of Eden. When God came and called to Adam, asking him where he was, Adam replied, 'When I heard your footsteps, I hid, because I am naked, and I am afraid.'

'Who told you that you are naked?' God asked. 'Have you eaten from the tree that I forbade?'

'Eve gave me the fruit, and I ate it,' Adam said.

'What have you done?' God admonished Eve

'The serpent tricked me,' Eve replied.

To punish the woman, God said, 'I will increase your labour and your pain, and you will bear children in pain. You will be eager for your husband, but he will be your master.'

And to man, God said. 'Because you listened to the woman and ate from the tree that I forbade, you will labour on the ground to get food, but, for the rest of life, the ground will grow thorns and thistles. You will have to gain your bread by the sweat of your brow, until you return to the ground from which you were taken. Dust you are and to dust you will return.'

To punish the serpent, God said, 'Because of what you have done, I curse you. From now on, you will crawl on your belly and eat dust for the rest of life. I will make you and the woman enemies, and the enmity will continue in your offspring. They will forever crush your head under their feet, and you will forever strike at their heels.'

Then God banished Adam and Eve from the Garden of Eden.

SHESHA NAAG THE ENDLESS ONE

Ananta, the endless one; Shesha, that which remains after the world ends. Shesha-Ananta Naag is a serpent, pure white, like a seashell, and thousand-hooded, with a gem embedded in each of his hoods. When the universe is annihilated, and the cosmos rests in primordial matter, Vishnu lies in repose on the coils of this serpent in the middle of the primordial ocean. After one kalpa of 311.04 trillion human years, a thousand-petalled lotus emerges from Vishnu's navel and sitting in the lotus is Brahma. As Vishnu, reclining on Shesha-Ananta, dreams the world, Brahma scribes it.

Shesha Naag was the first born among the sons of Kadru, who was the mother of a thousand snakes. She and her sister, Vinata, who was the mother of the sunbirds, Aruni and Garuda, placed a wager to guess the colour of the divine horse, Uchchaihshravas; the loser was to be the other's slave for five hundred years. To win the wager Kadru deceived her sister by having her snake sons braid themselves in the tail of the white horse so that he appeared black.

Aggrieved by the deception perpetrated by his mother and siblings, Shesha Naag disassociated himself from them and, assuming his human form, immersed himself in austere penance for hundreds of years, living in the mountains, subsisting only on air. By the time Brahma manifested before him to grant him a boon, Shesha Naag's human body actually looked like a snake's, with his long-knotted hair, shrivelled skin, dried sinews, and sunken eyes. The boon that Shesha asked from Brahma was to be delivered from his treacherous snake relatives and his own snakeness. 'O best of snakes,' Brahma replied, 'the earth has become unsteady with its cities and seas and mountains and forests. Go underneath her and hold her up on your thousand hoods. That will be your deliverance.' Thus, Shesha Naag became the bearer of the earth.

Shesha Naag also guards Jatarupasila, the mountain summit from which the sun rises. Sitting before this mountain of golden rocks that rises thirteen yojana high from the northern shore of the ocean, the chiliadal-headed white serpent shines like the moon. He is clad in blue, and his eyes are as large as the petals of a lotus. Shading him, like a banner, is the golden palmyra tree with three boughs. This tree is the boundary of the eastern quarter, beyond which the sun makes its appearance every morning.

Shesha Naag was also Krishna's elder brother, Balarama, both born from a black and white hair from Vishnu's chest. He was a master wrestler, best of mace fighters, and the bearer of the plough. When Krishna's clansmen of Yadavas destroyed themselves in an inebriated brawl, Balarama walked away to spend the rest of his life in meditation. As he sat in yoga on the seashore, a powerful white gigantic snake with a thousand heads emerged from his mouth and glided to the ocean, where his cosmic brethren, the celestial serpents, washed his feet and accepted him back into the fold. And his human body perished.

But Shesha is Ananta—endless, eternal. He remains guarding the sun-mountain and holding up the earth on his thousand hoods, even today. The evidence is in a legend about the city of Delhi: it is believed that in the eleventh century, the Tomar king, Anangpal, brought a seven-metre tall iron pillar, considered to be Vishnu's dhvaja (standard), from Vidisha and installed it in Mehrauli to establish the first city of Delhi. When he had it planted in the ground, an astrologer told him that the pillar had been pushed in so deep that it sat on the head of the world serpent, Shesha Naag, who was holding up the earth. The Tomar king was told that as long as the pillar remained installed, the Tomars would rule this land. But, Anangpal, not believing the astrologer, had the pillar pulled out, only to discover its bottom slick with blood. Worried that he had brought calamity upon his kingdom, he ordered his men to replant it. The pillar went back into the hole, but it never again fit firmly and stood like a loose nail—dhilli killi. And that's how Dhilli (Delhi) got its name. This pillar is still there, in the courtyard of the Qutub Minar, still standing on the thousand hoods of Shesha Naag.

TAKSHAKA AN OPHIDIAN EPITOME

Takshaka is the most underrated serpent in Hindu mythology. He is overshadowed by his more famous siblings, Shesha and Vasuki, who gained recognition through their reverential association with the great Vedic gods, Vishnu and Shiva. Takshaka, on the other hand, rejected the Vedic mainstream and proudly upheld his distinct Naga identity of snakeness, to the extent that his defiance became instrumental in shaping many defining events: it was to subjugate Takshaka that one of the world's first genocides occurred, and it was Takshaka who was the first survivor of the genocide. Also, when Great Time was on the cusp of Dvapara and Kali yugas, it was this very serpent who rang in the Dark Age. Takshaka, whose name itself means chiseller, is the architect who designs the form of things to be.

Takshaka was the fifth born of Kadru's one thousand snake sons. Long-bodied, copper-toned, with blue gems shining in his hood, like a diadem, he was the most luminous of his creatrix Earth Mother Kadru's offspring. More virulent than any other serpent, he was also a healer, the curer of the deadliest of poisons—his own. In fact, even Dhanvantri, the physician of the gods, sought Takshaka's friendship to learn the antidote to snake poison, and he used Takshaka's snakeness as the stem for all his medicine, the snakeness that is also intertwined with Asclepius's staff, which the whole world recognizes as the symbol of medicine.

When Takshaka bit Raja Parikshit, Arjuna's grandson,

who inherited the throne of Hastinapur after the Pandavas' death, at that very moment, the Vedic dharma cow lifted her third hoof off the earth. This sacred cow stands with four hooves firmly planted on the earth at the beginning of time, when the universe is pure. Her hooves denote the measure of dharma in each of the four yugas, and with each hoof she lifts, dharma diminishes, and the yuga changes. Thus, with Takshaka's act of biting Parikshit, Kali Yuga arrived. Here is how the story played out.

Once, during a hunt, Raja Parikshit shot a deer, but, although the animal was wounded, it escaped. Searching for him, separated from his retinue, a thirsty and hungry Parikshit came upon a rishi in a cowshed and asked him for some water. But the rishi ignored him. Not knowing that the holy man was observing a vow of silence, the king was angered by his disregard, and, to punish him, he picked up a snake carcass with the end of his bow and garlanded the rishi with it.

This rishi, Shamika, had a seven-year-old son, Sringin. When he found out about the insult someone had heaped on his father, he took anointed water in the cup of his hand and spewed a curse: 'May he who has defiled my father with a dead snake be bitten on the seventh day by the king of snakes, Takshaka.'

Fearing the curse, Raja Parikshit ordered his architects to build a palace erected on one pillar to curtail access to it, and he surrounded himself with doctors and pharmacists, and also with Brahmins expert in snake and anti-snake mantras. Nothing happened for six days. On the seventh morning, Takshaka sent some of his cohort snakes disguised as Brahmins to the palace, bearing a gift of nourishing fruits for the raja, to wish him the best of health. Parikshit allowed the Brahmins entry and accepted their gift, even as he anxiously awaited the culmination of the day. When the sun began to set, and there was still no sign of Takshaka, Parikshit sat back against satin pillows with a sigh of relief. Then, he took up a rosy, red apple from the fruits that the Brahmins had brought and, with a smile of pure hubris, declared: 'If the curse is true, may Takshaka bite me now—right this minute.'

Even as his teeth sank into the juicy flesh of the apple, a big copper-coloured bug buzzed out from it and changed into six coppery feet of deadly Takshaka. Winding himself around the raja's neck, the snake bit the scion of the Bharata clan, killing him instantly. Just at that moment, Great Time shifted into Kali Yuga.

◆

Takshaka once stole gold earrings from a rishi called Utanka, for no apparent reason other than the fact that gold is a treasure that belongs to the snakes, and since snakes and Brahmins have a long-standing enmity, Takshaka could not abide to see the Brahmin in possession of what was rightfully his. Taking the earrings, Takshaka burrowed deep into the ground and disappeared into Patala, the netherworld that is the home of snakes. But Rishi Utanka had acquired the earrings to pay his guru dakshina, so he urgently needed them back. With Indra's help, he managed to gatecrash Patala and retrieve the earrings. However, his anger at the snake still simmered, so he went to Raja Janamejaya, who had become ruler of the Kuru kingdom after Parikshit and, revealing to him the story of how his father had been killed, commanded him to avenge his father's death and destroy Takshaka. At that time, Janamejaya himself was searching for Takshaka for another reason: in a recent battle, he had won Takshaka's city, Takshashila, but he had been unable to subjugate the Naga. When he learned from Utanka that his father's killer was also Takshaka, Janamejaya swore to wipe out the entire Naga race. He organized a great fire sacrifice, a holocaust, to exterminate all the snakes. This is how the Mahabharata begins.

Sitting before the fire altar, as Janamejaya's priests chanted magnetizing mantras, calling out each naag by name, the snakes were yanked out of their lairs, one by one, and hurled into the flames. Thousands of snakes perished in that genocide. When Takshaka was called, he was in Indra's heaven, demanding the gods to stop the massacre. Snatched out of heaven by the magic of the mantras, he began to plummet earthward. But then, suddenly, his body stopped falling, and he hung suspended in midair. Looking down, he saw his nephew, Astika, who was the son of his snake sister, Jaratkaru, and a Brahmin, also named Jaratkaru, had arrived at the yajna and persuaded Janamejaya to cease the sacrifice. Hence, Takshaka lived.

This is how the Mahabharata ends: a race extermination aborted by a saviour of mixed race. And Takshaka, who gives form to things, saved by a boy called Astika, whose name means, 'Is'.

PAKHANGPA THE GUARDIAN PYTHON

Pakhangpa is a python-dragon guardian king of the Meitei and Chothe people of Manipur. He makes rain and thunder, and his colours are visible in the rainbow. Having the ability to appear and disappear at will, he appears at one spot and then vanishes into the earth, only to appear in another spot far away. He lives as a human, but, at night, he transforms into a divine python to save and protect his people from the lower gods, especially from the ferocious tiger king, Kamkeirang.

According to Chothe oral history, Pakhangpa once promised his people that he would come and dwell among them when they were settled and living a prosperous life. He did come to live with them, but they did not recognize him. One day, he suddenly appeared as a handsome young man before Daishin, the daughter of Chief Yulung Surou, when she was working in the jhum field. The two fell in love, and Daishin began to meet him clandestinely. Soon she became pregnant, and her father found out. When he asked her who her lover was, she could not tell him, because she had no idea; she did not even know if he was human or a demigod. To determine the identity of the being who had impregnated his daughter, Surou gave Daishin a potion made from turmeric, garlic, ginger, and snail, and told her to pour it on him. At their next meeting, when Daishin did as her father had asked, her lover's body began to burn. Daishin screamed, and the young man rushed to a nearby stream and jumped in. Hearing Daishin's screams, Joushin, Daishin's younger sister, who was also tending the jhum field, looked that way and caught a glimpse of a python's tail disappear in the water. After that Daishin was forbidden to leave the house, but she escaped many times to look for her lover in the neighbouring villages. She never found him; however, he often came in her dreams and assured her that he would always protect her and their baby.

Daishin gave birth to a son, whom she named Thangmei. But, because he had a strange, tail-like protrusion at the base of his spine, he was nicknamed Meingai (tail-man). People in the village called him illegitimate, which caused Daishin's father so much shame that he tried to kill the boy. He made three attempts, but each time the python saved his son in some mysterious way. Finally, Chief Surou banished his daughter.

Before Daishin left the village with her son, her father gave her one last gift—a hen and a rooster. 'Wherever the rooster crows, make that place your home,' he told her. It is believed that Daishin and young Thangmei went north, and, near Langthabal, on a small hillslope, the rooster crowed. That is where Daishin settled down with her son. However, when the inter-tribal wars broke out in the northern region, they had to move south, and they began to live in the village of Moirang.

In the course of time, Thangmei became a great leader of men, and, after the death of King Thangwai Kongding, he became the monarch. According to legend, he ruled in the fourth century and was the greatest of kings, consolidating all the small kingdoms in the south, and then marching north to subjugate other kings. Thus, he became the first sovereign ruler of the entire Manipur valley. He came to be known as Pakhangpa, and the Meitei believe that it is he who created their seven salais (clans). From then on, every king of Manipur assumed the title of Pakhangpa, and the looped dragon python, representing him, became heraldic for the kingdom of Manipur.

Pakhangpa's mystical form is called Paphal. There are three hundred and sixty-five diagrammatic illustrations of Paphal in the ancient manuscript of *Paphal Lambuba,* and they are all deities of nature, presiding over rivers, lakes, hills, caves, and floating islands of Manipur.

The Paphal python is also the divine existence in the human body.

MANDEHA THE SANDHILL

Shalmali Island, which is the abode of the sunbird, Garuda, is surrounded by red waters. On the island is a giant Kuta Shalmali (silk cotton) tree and mountains as high as the sky. Hanging suspended from the peaks of these mountains, like gigantic golden bats, are creatures so immense, they reach from mountaintop to the waters below. These are Mandehas. At dawn every morning, magnetized by the sun's rays, they raise their heads up till they are scorched to death. Then the consecrated water that holy men sprinkle in their morning rituals and the gayatri mantras they utter release the sun's hold on the Mandehas, and drop into the sea. As soon as they feel the cooling touch of the wine-red waves, they come back to life and climb up the mountains again to hang suspended from the mountain peaks. Day after day, the Mandehas are burnt to death by the sun and are resurrected by the water.

In the Ramayana, Sugriva's monkeys encounter these Mandehas when, searching for Sita, they scour the regions of Yavadwipa and Shalmali Island in the Red Sea.

◆

Yavadwipa is modern day Java, and it is believed that Shalmali Island may be Fraser Island on the southeastern coast of Queensland in Australia. Here the silk cotton trees grow to eighty feet. On the island is Lake Boomanjin, whose water is stained red from the tannin of the tea trees that grow around it. Fraser Island is also known for its sand-blown hills—dunes that rise to over two hundred metres and slowly shift, the sand in them moving like a creaturely mass from the peak to the beach below.

BHRAMARI THE BEEHIVE GODDESS

When Goddess Adi Shakti took the form of Bhramari, her body became a beehive. Swarms of bees emanated from her and spread in the four quarters. Mountain peaks, glens, forests—all became abuzz, and the sky became overcast with a fluttering black cloud.

The Goddess assumed this form to destroy the daitya, Aruna, who had received a boon from Brahma that his death could not be caused by war, weapons, man or woman, biped or quadruped, or even the combination of the two. Confident that this boon had made him invincible, Aruna, with his army of daityas, began to destroy the abodes of celestials and the yajnas of Brahmins. Unable to defeat him, the gods sought the Goddess's help.

When Adi Shakti manifested before the gods, she was wearing a garland that was shimmering and vibrating on her chest, and her fists were full of black bees. Innumerable bees were also swarming around her, humming the syllabic vibration of Hrim[11], which is Prakriti's force. By the time the Goddess reached the daityas, her whole body had become a beehive, buzzing with hundreds and thousands of black bees, that were neither weapons, nor man or woman, nor biped or quadruped, or even the combination of the two. They attacked the daityas, not in battle, but in the way bees attack those who destroy their beehives. The daityas were rendered

---

[11] The Hrimkara Mantra is the seed mantra, the primordial vibration.

helpless; they could not use their weapons, nor could they fight off the invasion in any other way. Stung repeatedly, they fell on the ground and died. When the destruction of the daityas was complete, all the bees flew back to the Goddess and were instantly absorbed by her iridescent being.[12]

---

[12] When the Hrimkara Mantra takes visible form, there is a burst of dazzling colours.

SHAMIR THE STONE-CUTTING WORM

Shamir is a worm, the size of a grain of barley. Its gaze is so sharp that it can cut through stone, iron, and diamond. When King Solomon built the First Temple in Jerusalem, he used a shamir to cut the stones. Because it was a temple of peace, he did not want to use any tools that engender violence.

The shamir has existed from the time of Moses. It was one of the ten wonders created by Yahweh on the eve of the first Sabbath. Moses himself used this worm to engrave the names of the twelve tribes of Israel on the breastplate of the high priest. But, after that, the shamir disappeared, and no one knew where it was. Some said it was hidden in paradise, and only Asmodeus, who is the king of earthly spirits and the prince of demons, knew where it was. Because Solomon needed the shamir for his temple, he brought Asmodeus under his control and made him reveal the worm's whereabouts. He discovered that it had been entrusted to the angel of the sea, and that angel had entrusted it to the moorhen. Hence, Solomon sent his aides to search for the shamir in the marshes, where the moorhen lives. They found it, caught it with cunning, and brought it to Solomon.

After Solomon used the shamir to build his temple in Jerusalem, he wrapped it up in wool and stored it in a container made of lead; its gaze is so sharp and fiery that any other container would have burst and disintegrated.

◆

In the Holy Qur'an, the shamir is called the 'worm of the earth.' It is mentioned in the story of Prophet Sulaiman's death. The prophet was an overseer of incarcerated jinns, who were building the temple. When he died, he was standing in the temple site, holding his staff. He remained leaning against the staff for almost a year. That whole time, the jinns continued to toil, thinking that the prophet was still alive. Then a worm of the earth gnawed through the staff, till it broke, and Sulaiman's body fell to the ground. That is when the jinns realized that their warden was dead, and they were free to escape.

When Nebuchadnezzar destroyed Solomon's Temple, the shamir disappeared from earth. The year was 586 BCE.

THE CATERPILLAR MAN

Once upon a time a caterpillar saw two girls. Changing itself into a man, he went to their house to visit them.

'Come and pick flowers with us in the forest,' the girls said to him.

'Fine,' he said. But, on the day of the assignment, he did not show up. The girls waited for him. All they saw was a caterpillar on a branch of a tree, lifting its tail and striking the flowers until they dropped to the ground.

Later that day, the caterpillar man went to visit the girls in their house again.

'Why didn't you come to pick flowers?' they asked. 'We waited for you.'

'I did come,' he replied. 'I even picked flowers for you. Didn't you get them?'

'All we saw was a caterpillar breaking the flowers with its tail.'

'That was me,' he said.

The girls were shocked and didn't want anything more to do with him. They tried to push him out of the house, but he refused to leave. So they killed him. Soon after, one of the girls also died.

This is the tale of the Caterpillar Man that the Ao Nagas tell.

ANTS—TEACHERS OF HUMILITY

SOLOMON AND THE ANT

Once, by chance, Solomon strayed into a valley of ants. As he strolled through it, he heard one of the ants ordering the others to quickly hide. Wondering why the little creatures were hiding, he summoned the ant that had issued the order. 'Who are you?' he asked, 'And why did you tell the others to hide?'

'I am the queen of ants,' she replied. 'I told my ants to hide so that they will not be crushed under the feet of your soldiers.'

'If you are the queen, then let me ask you a question,' Solomon said.

'I'll answer only if you pick me up and place me on your palm,' the ant replied.

Bending over, Solomon picked up the queen of ants and placed her on his palm. Then he asked his question: 'Is there any one greater than I in this whole world?'

'Yes, there is,' said the ant. 'I am.'

Solomon laughed. 'How is that possible?' he asked.

'If I were not greater than you, God would not have led you here and have you bend over to lift me into your palm.'

Solomon threw the ant to the ground and said, 'Do you know who I am? I am King Solomon.'

'Whoever you are—king or Solomon, you are of this earth, like the rest of us. No less, no more.'

Solomon left the valley of the ants, humbled and ashamed.

INDRA AND THE ANTS

Once, in the vainglory of his triumph over the asuras, Indra commanded Vishvakarma, the divine architect, to construct a palace for him that would truly reflect his eminence. Vishvakarma created design after design; however, not one of them met Indra's approval. Finally, exasperated by his pompousness, Vishvakarma sought Vishnu's help.

To teach the king of gods a lesson in humility, Vishnu disguised himself as a Brahmin boy and came to his palace. 'See those ants?' Vishnu asked Indra, pointing to a row of ants crawling across the floor in single file. 'Each one was an Indra in his time. Like you, each, by virtue of great deeds, became the king of gods, and each one, in subsequent rebirths, became an ant through arrogance and lack of virtue. These ants hold a secret that you should know, but you must choose to know it.'

Shocked, Indra watched the ants crawling across the floor of his palace, and he was filled with fear. 'What is the secret?' he asked Vishnu in a trembling voice.

'The secret is that life is a cycle of birth and rebirth, and in this cycle, each being is bound by his or her karma. Suffering the consequence of their own good and evil karmas, people get snared in this cyclicity. This is the secret—the wisdom that dispels the darkness of ignorance.'

Humbled, Indra decided to give up his heavenly palaces and become an ascetic to gain wisdom. Then, Brihaspati, the priest of the gods, explained to him the true virtue of life: 'The ideal existence is balance,' he said. 'Enjoy life but with the knowledge that it is your own karma that can make you an Indra or an ant.'

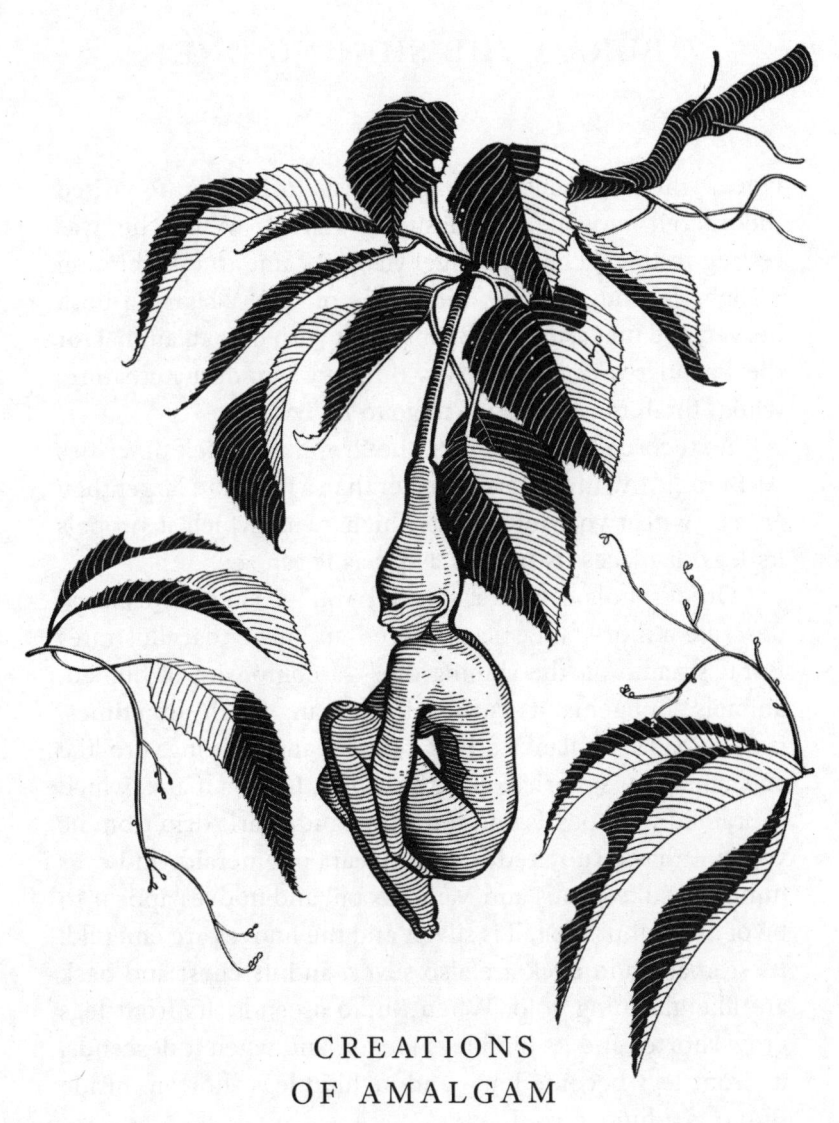

CREATIONS
OF AMALGAM

BURAQ THE SHINING ONE

Once, when Prophet Muhammad was in Mecca, he visited the sacred mosque, Al-Masjid al-Haram. While he was resting in the Ka'ba, the angel Gabriel came to take him on a Night Journey to show him some of Allah's signs in both heaven and on earth. Gabriel brought with him an animal for the Prophet to ride. This was Buraq, a wondrous creature, whom Ibrahim used to ride to go to Ka'ba.

As recorded by Ibn Ishaq, the Prophet himself describes Al-Buraq: 'A white animal, smaller than a mule but larger than an ass, with two wings on its thighs with which it propels its legs. It places its hooves as far as it can see.'

Other scholars, such as the Sufi Abu'l-Qasim al-Qushayri, describe a more fantastic creature—an image that illustrates Buraq's name of 'the shining one'—a composite of human, animals, and gems. Its face is of a human, which sometimes, is a woman's; its flanks are of a horse; and its wings are like an eagle's, but spherical, like the moon. It has a mane, which is braided with pearls and red coral, and pearls drip from its wings. It has a ruby red forehead, ears of emerald, and eyes luminous, like Venus and Mars. Its tail and hooves appear to be of a cow, but the tail is silver, and the hooves are emerald. Its stomach and neck are also silver, and its chest and back are like gleaming gold. When Buraq ascends, its front legs grow shorter and its hind legs longer, and when it descends, its front legs become long, and its hind legs shorten. Inside Buraq is a human soul.

For others, this description is apocryphal. However, regardless of how it is described, there is no doubt that it was Buraq who took the Prophet on his Night Journey. In the Surah Al-Isra, the Qur'an attests, 'Glory to (Allah) Who did take his servant for a journey by night from the Sacred Mosque [of Makkah] to the Farthest Mosque [Majid al-Aqsa of Jerusalem].' The rest of the story is revealed in the Hadith and by Ibn Ishaq:

> As soon as the Prophet got on Al-Buraq's back, it took off, and only stopped at Al-Masjid al-Aqsa in Jerusalem. The Prophet dismounted and tied Buraq with a golden chain to a ring in the wall that was already there from the time of the earlier prophets, who had also used it to tie Buraq. Then a ladder was brought to Muhammad, the kind of ladder that a dying man sees when death is upon him. Muhammad climbed this ladder with Gabriel, and they arrived at the Gate of Heaven, which is also called, the Gate of Watchers. Here Isma'il, who was in charge, asked Gabriel if Muhammad had been given a mission. 'Yes,' replied Gabriel, and Isma'il allowed the two to enter, wishing the Prophet well.
>
> Inside the gates, Gabriel first took Muhammad to see hell, and then he showed him the seven heavens. At the entrance of each heaven was an angel guarding the gate, and each one asked Gabriel the same question—whether Muhammad had been given a mission. In these heavens, Muhammad met Adam, Jesus, Joseph, Enoch, Aaron, Moses, and Abraham, and in the seventh heaven he reached the throne of

the Lord. When the Lord touched Muhammad, his heart trembled. But the All-knowing and Merciful Lord patted him on the shoulder and then laid upon him the duty of fifty prayers a day.

When the Prophet was on his way back, Moses stopped him and asked him how many prayers had been laid upon him.

'Fifty,' the Prophet replied.

'Go back and request the Lord to reduce the number,' Moses advised. 'Because the weight of the prayers will be too much for the people.'

Muhammad returned to the Lord and had the number of prayers reduced. But when he met Moses again, the prophet sent him back to request more leniency. Moses sent Muhammad back to the Lord numerous times to make the same plea, and each time the Lord reduced the number, till only five prayers remained for the whole day and night. Moses would have had that number lowered, as well, but Muhammad was too ashamed to return to the Lord to request for more concession. Hence, five prayers a day became tradition. But he who performs the five prayers in faith and trust receives the reward of fifty prayers.

After his journey to the heavens, the Prophet came back to Jerusalem, and, mounting Buraq, he returned to Mecca, just before daybreak. This Night Journey and Ascension, this Mi'raj of Prophet Muhammad on the twenty-seventh night of the month of Rajab in the year before the Hijrah is a spiritual journey of the human soul so that Allah's signs may be made clear to man. And Buraq, the shining one, who carried the Prophet on its back through this Journey, is like a prayer on which the journey is made.

NARIPHON THE PLANT WOMEN

In Himavata is a mythical mountain called Meru that is surrounded by a forest of trees. The fruit that these trees bear is young maidens—Nariphon. They emerge from pods, feet first, and grow about eight inches long in the form of a beautiful woman, hanging from the branches on stems attached to their heads. They remain in bloom for a week, and if they are not picked in those seven days, they fall to the ground and shrivel up. These maidens have the internal organs of a human, but they have no bones. They also have magical powers and possess spirits that sing and dance; that is why they are often picked by the celestial musicians, the gandharvas.

The tale of the Vessantara Jataka has given rise to folklore, especially in Thailand, that explains why these trees bear women: in his last incarnation, before he was born as Siddhartha Gautama, the Buddha was born as Vessantara, the son of Sanjaya, king of Sivi. Having a generous soul, Prince Vessantara gave away everything to the poor and needy, including the white elephant that was born at the time of his birth and ensured prosperity. Afraid that he would impoverish the land with this unceasing generosity, the people of Sivi exiled the prince, along with his children, Jali and Kanhajina, and his wife, Maddi. Living in exile, Maddi would often go to the forest to gather food and water for her family. One day, she discovered sixteen makali beru trees, from which, instead of fruit, hung small, beautiful makaliphool or nariphool maiden-flowers. These trees had been planted by Indra as a distraction to protect Maddi from the roving eyes of forest dwelling hermits. They were also a test to gauge whether disciplined hermits had conquered lust. If a hermit, who had reached the pinnacle of meditation, picked a nariphool and had intercourse with her, he lost all his merit.

In Indian folk legends, the Nariphon is Narilatha, a flower in the shape of a woman, and it blooms on Himavata every twenty years. But these flowers can only be seen by the most highly evolved of rishis, especially so, because Himavata is not accessible to ordinary men. However, a time will come when these flowers will no longer be visible, even to holy men, because when the Buddha's teachings are lost, the forest where Nariphon grows will disappear.

ADNE SADEH THE HUMAN PLANTS

Adne Sadeh was a human that sprouted from the ground. It had a human's face, body, hands, and feet, but it grew like a gourd or melon, attached to the earth with its umbilical cord that served as a stem. Because it could only move as far as its stem allowed, it fed on the fruits and vegetables that grew around it and on any small animals that happened to come within its reach. It could live a long time, but if it was plucked, it died instantly.

The Talmud calls Adne Sadeh 'the man of the mountain'. In Jewish folklore, it is called Fedua. In earlier times, people thought it was a lamb plant with prophetic abilities, so they harvested it by severing its uterine stem with arrows or darts, and they used its bones for divination.

Some say that Adne Sadeh was God's failed attempt at creating human beings before he created Adam. That is why it existed only till the Flood. Then God just let it drown.

DADHIKRAVANA THE BIRD-HORSE AND HAYAGRIVA THE HORSE-HEADED

DADHIKRAVANA

Hymns in the Rig Veda describe Dadhikravana as a bird-horse; not a composite, but a stallion analogous to a falcon and hamsa: 'A mighty steed,' like a 'a hamsa honed in flight,' and 'bound by the neck, flanks, and mouth.' This 'vigorous Courser, full of bounties and shining like Agni, moves people to exertion and prolongs their life. He is invoked at dawn by the priests and he dwells 'in the noblest places, amid men, in truth, in sky; he is the holy Law' (4.39-40). Thus, it appears that Dadhikravana is, perhaps, a zoomorphication of the morning sun.

The Katha Upanishad uses the exact same words as the Rig Veda to describe Dadhikravana. However, here, the bird-horse is a metaphor of the Self.

He is the swan, hamsa (the moving sun) in the holy heaven, in the middle region he is the air all pervasive, by the altar he is the offering priest, in the house he is the guest...in men does he live and in gods and in truth, and in the sky. He is born of water, he is born of earth, he is born of sacrifice and of the mountains—that truth, that great (2.2.2).

Hence, Dadhikravana is the steed, the hamsa, the dawn sun—all emblems that represent the Self.

HAYAGRIVA

Once the gods, desiring to perform a sacrifice, sought Vishnu, who is a master of sacrifice and sacrifice itself. However, at that time, Vishnu, exhausted from the battle between the devas and asuras, was reposing in deep yoga. His head was resting on one end of the strung bow, while its other end was planted firmly in the ground. To awaken him, Brahma devised a plan. He created Vamri, the termite, and asked her to eat away the lower limb of the bow that was planted in the ground. But Vamri refused; she was afraid to awaken the Great Lord, so the gods promised her a share in the sacrifice. With Vamri's gnawing, the wood of the bow snapped, but the noise was so loud that it reverberated throughout the world; the oceans convulsed, violent winds blew, mountains shook, ominous meteors fell, the sun sank into the horizon, and the gods themselves squeezed their eyes shut in fear. When they opened their eyes, they saw Vishnu's body seated on the ground, but it was headless. They searched for Vishnu's head everywhere, but it was nowhere to be found. In despair, the gods went to Devi to beg for her help. She told them that when the bow broke, the bowstring sliced off Vishnu's head, and it flew into the air and then fell into the salty ocean.

'Why did this happen?' the gods wanted to know.

'It was a result of Lakshmi's curse,' Devi informed them.

'Once, Vishnu laughed at Lakshmi for no apparent reason. "Why did you laugh at me?" Lakshmi asked him, but when Narayana gave no explanation, the Goddess became angry and cursed him: "May your head fall off." What has happened is the fulfilment of her words. But there is another reason, as well: it is to destroy Hayagriva, the daitya. Through arduous tapasya, he has received a boon from Brahma that because his name means "horse-necked", he can only be killed by someone whose head is of a horse. Brahma's boon has made Hayagriva invincible, and he is oppressing the devas and rishis. Now it is time to destroy him, and only Vishnu can accomplish this task. However, before he can undertake it, he must become the one with a horse's head—Hayashiras. That is why his own head has been severed.'

'But where can we find a suitable horse's head for Vishnu?' the gods asked worriedly.

'Do not fear. His head will be crafted by Vishvakarma.'

Thus, the divine architect, Vishvakarma, made a customized horse's head for Vishnu and grafted it onto his body, and, in that horse-headed form, Vishnu destroyed Hayagriva. Then he took the daitya's name and himself came to be known as Hayagriva.

YALI A SYNTHESIS IN STONE

Yali is carved in granite on the pillared columns of Hindu temples.

Often monolithic, ranging in height from seven feet to twenty-two feet, the Yali usually has a lion's head and body, an elephant's tusks, and a serpent's tail. Its eyes bulge, and its lips draw back in a snarl to reveal long, sharp teeth. The term, 'yali', derives from the Sanskrit 'vyala', which refers to a ferocious beast of prey.[13] Vyalas were often depicted in Kushana art sculptures of Mathura from the first to third centuries CE. The Yali, adopting characteristics from the vyala, began to appear in the architecture of the sixteenth century Vijayanagara empire and continued to be portrayed through the Nayak period of the eighteenth century.

Most Yalis are ithyphallic and have a leonine head. Sometimes the lion's head is replaced by that of an elephant, or a horse, or a dog, and occasionally, even a human. They are normally found at the entrance of temples, where they stand as dwarapalas, protective guardians of the gate, as in the Vijaya Vittala Temple in Hampi. Often, they also line the aisles of mandapa halls and processional corridors, such as in Ranganathaswamy Temple in Srirangam and the thousand-

---

[13]The *Samarangana Sutradhara*, an eleventh century encyclopaedic work on Indian architecture, attributed to Raja Bhojadeva of Dhara, enumerates sixteen vyalas: deer, vulture, parrot, rooster, lion, tiger, wolf, goat, rhinoceros, beer, horse, buffalo, dog, monkey, elephant, and donkey. But no matter in what form the vyala is depicted, it is always ferocious.

pillared hall in Meenakshi Amman Temple in Madurai. They can be seen at the base of pillars as well, exuding preternatural energy, as though they are anchoring the whole temple, as in the Airavateshvara Temple in Darasuram in Thanjavur; or they are placed atop pillars, stabilizing them with their pressing force, as in the Vidyashankara Temple in Sringeri. Occasionally, a Yali is himself anchored on a makara, the crocodile vyala. And, some Yalis, such as those in the Jalakandeshwara Temple of Vellore and in the Mukteshwar Temple of Bhubaneswar, have human warriors riding them. In this depiction, their front legs are raised, as though in attack.

Yali is, perhaps, inspired by Vishnu's Narasimha avatar, who erupted from a pillar to protect Prahalad from his asura father, Hiranyakashipu. Grasping the asura on his lap, Narasimha tore him to shreds with his fierce claws and teeth. However, in folklore, Yali himself is subdued by Narasimha. Hence, in some Vishnu festivals, such as in the temple of Sri Lakshmi Narasimha Swamy in Mangalagiri, the idol of Narasimha rides a Yali vehicle.

Ironically, a ferocious, elephant-headed, lion-bodied Yali is also the ride of the wise and calm planet, Mercury—Budha, who is lord of planets. Budha understands composited dualities as no other. He married the transgendered Ila, and in Jyotisha, he rules the paired zodiacal signs, Mithun, (Gemini), and the feminine-natured Kanya (Virgo). Budha is also that part of us which knows; he is our intellect. Thus, with Budha riding the powerful Yali, Yali himself becomes a synthesis of power and knowledge.

CHALKYDRI THE ANGELS OF THE SUN

Chalkydri are serpent-angels of the flying sun. Their feet and tail are of a lion, their head is of a crocodile, and their size is nine measures. They each have twelve angel wings, coloured luminescent purple, like a rainbow. Along with the Phoenix, the Chalkydri help pull the chariot of the sun through its twelve gates—six in the east and six in the west—that represent the twelve constellations of the zodiac.

Chalkydri live in the fourth heaven, which maps the course of the sun and the moon. Jerusalem is located here, as is the Holy Temple, where the angel Michael offers righteous souls in sacrifice at the Holy Altar.

When the sun rises each day, the Chalkydri burst into joyous song to announce to the world the arrival of the light-giver. This is the reason why, at dawn, birds flutter their wings and sing.

KINNARA—PERHAPS A MAN

The word Kinnara itself contains a question. Kim-Nara: Is it? Man.

Kinnaras are human-like; they are half man, half horse. They live on Mandara Mountain in the Himalaya, guarding Kubera's treasures, floating just a few fingers above earth and water. According to the *Chanda-Kinnara Jataka*, they feed on soma and live to be a thousand years. They anoint themselves with flower perfumes, eat pollen, clothe themselves in flower-gauze, swing in creepers, and sleep on flowerbeds. They are also celestial singers, and the summit of Meru constantly echoes with their honeyed, melodious songs.

Once the Bodhisattva was a Kinnara, living on Chanda Parbat with Yashodhra as a Kinnari named Chanda. One day, Brahmadatta, the king of Banaras, saw them sporting and singing. He desired the Kinnari, so he shot an arrow at the Kinnara. But the Kinnari's laments for her slain lover were so passionate that the king's desire turned cold and Indra's throne burned. The king of gods had to descend on the mountain to revive the Kinnara.

The *Bhallatiya Jataka* tells the story of how King Bhallatiya of Banaras once came upon a Kinnara and Kinnari weeping piteously on Gandhamadana Mountain. 'Why do you weep?' he asked them, and they told him about a night, six hundred and ninety-seven years ago: the Kinnari was gathering flowers when a great storm arose in the river and swept everything away. The Kinnara and Kinnari got separated and spent the night looking for each other. They found each other the following morning; however, the sorrow of that night of separation still lingered in their hearts and made them weep.

Kinnaras are eternal lovers. When Kamadeva goes on his missions of love, accompanied by his friend, Vasanta, Kinnaras tag along, because nothing pleases them more than watching love happen.

SHARABHA A SHIVA AVATAR

He looked like a colossal bird with wings and a beak, but his face was of a ferocious lion. A mane of long, matted hair, like serpents, swung from his head, and his beak-mouth hissed and snapped, revealing vicious fangs. He had four legs with powerful hooves and a thousand powerful arms with adamantine claws. His lion's body was as black as night, but his face was blazing like doomsday fire. And, perched on his head, tender, like the compassion of the Great God, was the crescent moon.

This was Sharabha, an incarnation that Shiva assumed to save Vishnu from himself.

When the arrogant daitya, Hiranyakashipu, oppressed the world and threatened the life of his own son, Prahalad, for being a Vishnu devotee, Vishnu took the form of the man-lion, Narasimha, to destroy the daitya. In the fury of battle, Narasimha threw Hiranyakashipu on his lap and tore open his stomach with his claws to devour his entrails and drink his blood.

When the daitya was slain, the universe rejoiced, but the gods were not at peace. Hiranyakashipu was dead, but the fiery rage of the divine beast who had been invoked in Vishnu had not abated. The gods knew that if this rage did not subside soon, it would destroy the universe. They also knew that the poison in the daitya's blood that Vishnu had consumed could not be digested and would rampage. Thus, the Preserver, who had incarnated into this terrible being, would himself annihilate what he was born to preserve. Then, what would become of the cosmic order?

To calm the man-lion, the gods sent Prahalad to him. After all, it was to save him that Vishnu had turned himself into the beast. The gods' strategy seemed to work; even in the fervour of violence, Narasimha embraced the boy with love. However, the passion to destroy still surged in him, and setting Prahalad aside, he roared again and rose up to decimate everything in his path. The devas then realized that the only one who could save the universe from Narasimha was Shiva. Going to the Great God, they eulogized him, reminding him of all the instances in times past when he had saved the universe from annihilatory forces as lethal as the poison, Halahala.

Accepting the devas' plea, Shiva invoked Virabhadra, his terrible form that had emerged during Daksha's sacrifice, when Sati had immolated herself. The unsubdued, the mighty, the pacifier of heated ones, the passionate Virabhadra became instantly manifest, dancing and leaping in joy, like the fire at the end of the kalpa. His three eyes shone, his hair was matted, and a crescent moon sat on his head, like a delicate silver ornament. He had no weapons, but he had fangs that were like splinters of Indra's lightning.

'Why have you summoned me?' Virabhadra asked Shiva.

'Go to Narasimha and conciliate him,' Shiva said. 'Convince him to abandon his anger. But if he is not convinced, show him my terrible form, and if he still resists, destroy him and bring me his head.'

Controlling his natural disposition of wrathfulness, Virabhadra went to Narasimha and spoke to him in a gentle tone: 'You are entrusted with the preservation of the universe,' he said. 'Whenever the earth is in misery, you incarnate to liberate people from distress. You are the origin of all living beings. You killed Hiranyakashipu for a purpose, and you took this incarnation to protect the world and Prahalad from him. Now that the world and Prahalad have been saved, you must give up this furious form and return to your benign self.'

But Narasimha would not be pacified. In fact, his anger intensified, and he roared, 'Go back to where you came from. I am going to annihilate the world. I am the greatest. Everyone, including the gods, is alive only by my favour; even the creator, Brahma, was born from the lotus of my navel. I am Kala, the final cause of destruction. I am the Death of Death.'

Seeing Narasimha filled with self-importance, Virabhadra laughed at him in disdain. 'After tearing apart just a single daitya, you roar pompously. Don't you know that the power you are bragging about has been endowed to you by the Great Lord, Shiva? This man-lion incarnation that you are flouting, like all your other incarnations, has been shaped by Him, as on a potter's wheel.'

After issuing this challenge, the form of Virabhadra became invisible and Shiva's splendour emerged from him, enveloping the earth and the sky. Neither golden nor fiery, neither lunar nor solar, it resembled neither lightning nor the moon; it was just brilliance, as it merged with Shiva. Then the Great God manifested as the Annihilator, Sharabha.

In comparison to Sharabha, Narasimha's lustre became no more than a glowworm's in the rays of the sun, and he cowered in fear. With a flutter of wings, Sharabha grabbed Narasimha with his beak and tore him from the navel up with his claws. Then, taking his own lion's tail, he wrapped his legs and hands with it. After that, like a vulture seizing a serpent, he caught him in his beak again and, lifting him up, flung him to the ground and beat him with his wings. The man-lion expired on the spot, and, finally, the peaceful essence of Vishnu was free.

Sharabha's work was done. Amidst hails of glory from the gods, he vanished. Then Virabhadra, who had become visible again, tore off the skin from the body of the felled Narasimha and cut off his head, and he carried these away to Himalaya. The lion hide on which the Great Lord sits in meditation on Mount Kailasha is that same peeled skin, and the biggest head in his necklace of skulls is that very same head.

GANDABHERUNDA A VISHNU AVATAR

To expel Narasimha, the destructive, rageful man-lion from Vishnu's being, Shiva took the winged form of the fearsome Sharabha. With his savage claws, Sharabha tore Narasimha from the navel up, and, binding him with his own lion's tail, smashed him on the ground to finish him.

But Narasimha did not die. He rose, seething in fury, and in the blink of an eye, his body transformed into a being even more ferocious than the man-lion and even more dreadful than Sharabha. This was Gandabherunda, a monstrous, eight-headed falcon. Each of its heads was a different animal's, and its legs and talons were longer and sharper than Sharabha's. For eighteen days Sharabha and Gandabherunda fought, tearing at feathers and flesh with their talons and beaks. Finally, Gandabherunda caught Sharabha's tattered body in his beak and crushed him to death.

◆

In many South Indian depictions, Gandabherunda is not eight-headed; it is a falcon with two heads. The source of both these descriptions is ambiguous, but the rock-cut sculptures in many temples in Karnataka make it evident that the two-headed Gandabherunda bird was a well-recognized tradition, especially in sixteenth-century Vijayanagara empire. In fact, it was such a significant and symbolic image, that it was adopted as the royal insignia by the kingdom of Mysore, and, later, when Karnataka was given statehood, it became a part of the state's emblem.

There is no specific Puranic narrative about Vishnu's transformation into Gandabherunda; however, the origin of this form can be traced to the Vedas and Puranas: the soma used in Vedic sacrifices was belived to have been brought by shyena birds, the falcons, from the mountains of the gandharvas. Soma is associated with the moon, and consequently, with Shiva. Also, 'bherunda', which means 'fearsome', is considered a form of Shiva. Hence, it is possible that Gandabherunda may initially have been a part of Shaivic traditions. However, since sacrificial altars were built in the shape of a falcon, and Vishnu himself is considered the lord of sacrifice, the affiliation may have shifted from Shiva to Vishnu. Additionally, Vishnu's vehicle, the sunbird Garuda, is amalgamated with Shyena in the Puranas, and this may have concretized Gandabherunda's Vaishnava affiliations.

Shaivic and Vaishnava sects had an acrimonious and retaliatory relationship, which is echoed in the enmity between Sharabha and Gandabherunda. Thus, Sharabha's victory over Narasimha may have been a Shaivic bid to gain the upper hand, but Gandabherunda's victory over Sharabha clinched Vaishnava supremacy.

This enmity is also seen as a natural chain of destruction in temple depictions: Gandabherunda bird of prey attacks a Sharabha; the Sharabha grabs a lion; the lion preys on an elephant, which fights a python; the python swallows a rat or an antelope. And watching this immense hierarchical order unfold is a small figure of man.[14]

---

[14]Stone panels showing this scenario are in in the Chennakeshava Temple at Belur and in the Jain Bucheshvara Temple at Koravangala.

NAVAGUNJARA A UNITY

Navagunjara is a nine-animal composite of Krishna's Universal Form. It was envisioned by Sarala Das, who is considered the author of the fifteenth-century Odia Sarala Mahabharata.

Here is how Navagunjara manifests in this epic: Agni, disguised as a Brahmin priest, requests Arjuna to summon Yudhishthira for an urgent matter, but Arjuna refuses. His elder brother is with Draupadi at that hour, and, as per the condition of the Pandavas' polyandrous marriage, the brothers have sworn not to disturb each other's private time with Draupadi, no matter the reason. And, if the oath is violated by any one of them, he is to go away for twelve years of exile as penalty. At Arjuna's refusal to fetch Yudhishthira, Agni threatens to burn the entire land. Fearful of Agni's wrath, Arjuna breaks the vow and goes into his elder brother's room to summon him. Then he leaves for twelve years of exile. Four years, six months, and thirteen days into exile, he is on Manibhadra Mountain, coating the string of his bow, when he sees a strange being frolicking in the foliage. It is an amalgam of nine creatures: its head is of a rooster, its throat is a peacock's, its body, complete with hump, is of a bull, its waist is that of a lion, and its tail is a snake. One of its legs is that of a tiger, another one has the hoof of a horse, the third is an elephant's leg, and the fourth is a human hand holding a lotus.

At first Arjuna is taken aback by this bizarre, illusionary

creature, the likes of which he has never seen. Then he surmises that this can be no other than Krishna who is playing a trick on him. To confirm this, Arjuna falls at the creature's feet and eulogizes Krishna. Sure enough, Krishna reveals himself in his Vishnu form.

This chimeric being is not in Vyasa's Mahabharata, nor is it in any other version of the epic; it only makes an appearance in Sarala Das's composition. Hence, one wonders: was Navagunjara simply a flight of Sarala Das's fancy, or was the poet conveying a deeper meaning? Was he making a statement through this creature? Sarala Das was a farmer, and most likely a Shudra. By creating Navagunjara, was he perhaps demonstrating that all beings, no matter their caste, reside in Krishna? Or, perhaps he was bemoaning the destruction of ecosystems resulting from the burning of forests, because immediately after the display of Navagunjara, Arjuna accompanies Agnideva to Khandava forest and puts it to flame, slaughtering all the animals in it and destroying numerous medicinal herbs and minerals.

Worthy of note is the fact that unlike in Vyasa's Mahabharata, where Krishna and Arjuna together destroy Khandava forest, in Sarala Das's version, Krishna refuses to join Arjuna in bringing about the carnage. By removing Krishna from this situation was Sarala Das rescuing the divine from a grave ethical transgression? Also worth noting is the human hand holding a lotus in the image. The lotus symbolizes man's potential to achieve inner perfection by controlling sense organs, which is the core teaching of the Bhagavad Gita. Perhaps, Navagunjara was Sarala Das's visual encapsulation of this message.

Whatever may have inspired Sarala Das to create such a

fantastical creature, it clearly held great significance, because even though Navagunjara's appearance in the epic is fleeting, its role in Odia traditions has been long-lasting. Even today, Odia artists continue to render it in their work; the nine-creatured Navagunjara is a frequent motif in Pattachitra art.

HARAPPAN CHIMERA[15]

Among thousands of seals that have been discovered in the archeological sites of the Indus Valley, many are of a square stamp, dated, perhaps, 2800 BCE, and depicting a chimera—a composite being with characteristics of seven or eight animals.

The fired steatite engravings show a creature that had the hindquarters and legs of a tiger with sharp-clawed paws. Its body is slim, like that of a unicorn, emphasizing its penile maleness. His neck is banded, giving the impression of a thick mane, perhaps, of the makhor, the mountain goat of the Hindukush. His ears, raised and alert, are also of the makhor, and its forelegs, too, with fur around the joints and hooves, resemble the mountain goat. The two large, serrated horns on its head are curved like crescent moons—similar to a makhor's, as well. It has a tail, which is not really a tail; it is an erect cobra with a distended hood, ready to strike. And its face is of a human, or something like a human, with unnaturally bulging eyes. Also, in the place of a nose, it has a trunk, sort of elephantine, but it is more in the shape of a hanging human arm ending in a human hand.

What an odd creature this is—like a random patchwork of beings, or an amalgam by design. Was this chimera pure

---

[15]All the information about the Harappan Chimera is from an article by Dennys Frenez and Massimo Vidale, 'Harappan Chimaeras as "Symbolic Hypertexts": Some Thoughts on Plato, Chimaera and the Indus Civilization', *South Asian Studies*, Vol. 28, No. 2, 2012, pp. 107–30.

imagination, or was it a creature of myth? Was it a merging of divinities—a unity of different faiths? Or was each component a synecdoche of individuated belief systems? Some scholars believe it was an economic imperative: a chart of symbols representing chieftains in the trading ports of the Indus Valley. If so, was it an emblem of oligarchy?

There are no answers to these questions. The Indus script is still undeciphered, and the seals that speak of the society and culture depict a language that is incomprehensible. But, perhaps, this creature can be understood in today's terminology of computing. Modern scholars are calling it an early form of hypertext. They believe that each chimeric part may have been a link to knowledge that the Indus Valley people had access to. Sadly, these hyperlinks are no longer active, but, maybe, one day, they will be clickable again.

ACKNOWLEDGEMENTS

I wrote *Adbhut* in the isolation of the pandemic. Therefore, those I want to thank for this book are my dear ones who kept me, and each other, sane during that time.

Dear all, thank you for keeping us connected to the outside world by sharing photos of your spring gardens and sky balconies and window-sized views of sunny neighbourhoods. Thank you for zoom-linking the tribe every month just so we could see each other's faces and clink glasses of wine in cyberspace. Thank you for celebrating us, even though our hair was becoming its true grey, our waistlines were increasing, our eye bags were getting heavier, and our hearts were breaking at losing yet another loved one to Covid.

Dear Aienla, I am very grateful to you, as well. You anchor my writing life.

And Bena, your artwork takes my breath away. Thank you for making this book come alive.

SOURCES

CREATURES OF THE SKY

1. Simurgh the Soul's Reality

Abolqasem, *Shahnameh: The Persian Book of Kings*, tr. Dick Davis, New York: Penguin Books, 2001, p. 226.
Farid ud-Din Attar, *The Conference of Birds*, tr. Afkham Darbandi and Dick Davis, London: Penguin Books, 1984.
Rashn Yasht, v. 17, tr. James Darmesteter, *Sacred Books of the East* (American edn), New York: Christian Literature Co., 1898.
Rigveda, IV.26.4.
Warharan Yasht, v. 41, tr. James Darmesteter, *Sacred Books of the East* (American edn), New York: Christian Literature Co., 1898.

2. Ziz the Bird of Chaos

Howard Schwartz, *Tree of Souls: The Mythology of Judaism*, New York: Oxford University Press, 2004.
Nili Wazana, 'Anzu and Ziz: Great Mythical Birds in Ancient Near Eastern, Biblical, and Rabbinic Traditions', *JANES*, Vol. 31, Issue 1, 2009.

3. Kaka Bhasundi the Time-travelling Crow

Tulasidas, *Shri Ramacharitmanasa*, Uttarakand, 17–771.

4. Byangoma and Byangomi

Dakshinaranjan Mitra Majumdar, *Thakurmar Jhuli* (Bengali edn), 1907.

Rabindranath Thakur, 'Bhumika,' introduction in *Thakurmar Jhuli*, 1907.

5. Hiraman the Talking Parrot

A. G. Shirreff, *Padmavatī*, Royal Asiatic Society of Bengal, 1944.

Eberhard Fischer and Dinanath Pathy, 'Amorous Delight: The "Amarushataka" Palm Leaf Manuscript', Illustrated by the Master of Sharanakula (Orissa, India), *Artibus Asiae. Supplementum*, Vol. 47, 2006, pp. 1, 3–9, 11, 13–255.

Lal Behari Dey, 'The Story of a Hiraman.'

Piyush Pachak, 'Unique Parrot on the Verge of Extinction,' *The Tribune*, 1 June 2002.

Rumi, *The Masnavi*, tr. E. H. Whinfield, 1898, Internet Sacred Texts Archive.

Somadevabhatt, *Kathasaritsagara*, tr. Pandit Kedarnath Sharma Saraswat, Bihar Rashtrabhasha Parishad, 2005.

The Padumawāti of Malik Muhammad Jaisi, tr. G. A. Grierson and Mahamahopadhaya Sudhakara Dvivedi, Asiatic Society of Bengal, 1896.

6. Jatayu the Braveheart

Tulsidas, *Shri Ramacharitmanasa*, Aranyakanda, XV and XLIX–LI.

Yamini Nair, 'Jatayu in Kerala, Safe As a Rock!', *Hindustan Times*, 21 October 2018.

7. Peacock the Beautiful, the Sad

Marian Roalfe Cox, 'Introduction', *Introduction to Folk Lore*, London: David Nutt, 1895, p. 17.
Tulsidas, *Shri Ramacharitmanasa*, Uttarakanda, XVIII, 21–25.
Verrer Elwin, *Myths of Middle India*, Indian Branch, Oxford University Press, 1949.

8. Chitta Baaz

'Northern Goshawk', *All About Birds*, Cornell Lab of Ornithology.
'The State Bird of Punjab: Northern Goshawk', *Punjab ENVIS Newsletter*, Vol. 14, No. 3.
'White Falcon', *Sikh Wiki: Encyclopedia of the Sikhs*.
Look! This is Love: Poems of Rumi, tr. Annemarie Schimmel, Boston: Shambala Publications, 1996.
The Holy Qur'ān, tr. Abdullah Yusuf Ali, Surah 89:27–28.

9. The Chakora and His Love and Longing

'Panchhi Bawara', *Bhakt Surdas*, dir. Chaturbhuj Doshi, Singer, Khurshid Bano, Lyrics, D. N. Madhok, 1942.
Kabir, doha, 'Lagi lagan chute nahi, jeebh chonch jari jaye/ Meetha kaha angaar mein, jaahi chakor chabaaye'.
Kazi Nazrul Islam, 'Khodaro Preme Sharabo Piye'.
Rahim, doha, 'Aho Sudhakara pyaare, neh nichor/ Dekhan hi ko tarsain nain chakor'.

10. Garuda the Devourer

The Garuda Purana, tr. Ernest Wood and S. V. Subrahmanyam, 1911, Internet Sacred Texts Archive.

Mahabharata, Adi Parva.

11. Phoenix—Reborn from Its Own Ashes

'Second Book of Enoch', *The Book of the Secrets of Enoch*, Internet Archive.
Howard Schwartz, *Tree of Souls: The Mythology of Judaism*, New York: Oxford University Press, 2004.
Louis Ginzberg, *Legends of the Jews* Vol. 1, available at <gutenberg.org>.
Philostratus, *Life of Apollonius*, 3.46-50, Livius, livius.org, pp. 111–135.
Wazana, 'Anzu and Ziz'.

CREATURES OF THE SEA

12. Matysa the Cosmic Fish

Mahabharata, Vana Parva.
Matsya Purana, 1-11-34.
Shatapatha Brahmana, 1-8, 1-6.

13. Leviathan the Sea Monster

'Leviathan and Behemoth', *Jewish Encyclopedia*.
Howard Schwartz, *Tree of Souls: The Mythology of Judaism*, New York: Oxford University Press, 2004.
The Bible, Psalm 74: 14, Isiah 27:1, Job 41, Psalm 104:26.

14. Makara the Immortal Crocodile

Ananda K. Coomaraswamy, *Yakshas* Part 2, Washington D. C.: Smithsonian Institution, Freer Gallery of Art, 1931, p. 55.

Asko Parpola, 'Beginnings of Indian and Chinese Calendrical Astronomy', *Journal of the American Oriental, Society*, Vol. 134, No. 1.

———, *The Roots of Hinduism: The Early Aryans and the Indus Civilization*, New York: Oxford University Press, 2015.

Mahabharata, Bhishma Parva.

Vishnudharmottar Purana, 3rd Khanda.

15. Kurma the World Tortoise

Mahabharata, Vana Parva.
Shatapatha Brahmana, Kanda VII, Fifth Adhyâya, 1–6.
Taittiriya Samhita, 5.2.8.

16. Timingila That Once Was

Caitanya-Caritamrta, Madhya-lila, 13.142.
Mahabharata, Vana Parva.
Tulsidas, *Shri Ramacharitmanasa*, Yudhakanda, 4, 97–102, 21–22, 22:1–50.

17. Varaha the Good and Evil Boar

Bhagavata Purana, 111.
Kalika Purana, 30.7
Tulsidas, *Shri Ramacharitmanasa*, Ayodhyakanda.
Vishnu Purana, 1.34.

18. The Golden Hamsa

'Hamsa Upanishad', *Sixty Upanishads of the Vedas*, ed. Paul Deussen, Vol. 2, New Delhi: Motilal Banarsidass Publishers, 1980.

Brihadaranyaka Upanishad, 4.3.12.
Shvetashwara Upanishad, 6.15.
Srimad Valmiki-Ramayana, Aryanakanda, XIV.
Stella Kramrisch, 'Image of Buddha from Gandhara', *Philadelphia Museum of Art Bulletin*, Vol. 61, No. 289, Spring, 1966, pp. 36–39.

19. Badava the Submarine Mare

Shiva Purana, Part 11, 48–50.

CREATURES OF THE EARTH

20. Behemoth the Land Monster

1 Enoch, 'Book of Noah', 58.
Louis Ginzberb, *The Legends of the Jews*, Vol. 5, Philadelphia: The Jewish Publication Society of America, 1925.
The Bible, Job 40:18.

21. The She-Camel

Tafsir Ibn Kathir, Vol 2. (Tafsir Al-Qur'an Al-Azim), Surah: 7, Al A'raf (part 8), Internet Archive.
The Holy Qur'ān, Surahs: 7-73-79; 26-141-158; 27; 49-50.

22. Akoman the Evil Mind

Denkard 8 and 9, tr. E. W. West, *Sacred Books of the East*, Oxford: Oxford University Press, 1897.
J. Duchesne-Guillemin, 'AKŌMAN,' Encyclopædia Iranica, I/7, pp. 728–729.
Major Ranft, *The Esoteric Codex: Zoroastrian Legendary*

Creatures (First edn), Lulu Press, 2015.

23. The Golden Mongoose

Derygk O. Lodrick, 'Man and Mongoose in Indian Culture.' *Anthropos*, Bd. 77, H. 1./2., 1982, pp. 191–214.
Elwin Verrier, *Myths of Middle India*, Internet Archive.
Vishnu Sharma, *Panchantantra*, 'Rash Deeds'.

24. The Dog That Guards the Judgement Bridge

Avesta: *Vendidad, Fargard VIII*, 16–17.
The Zend Avesta, Part 1: Vendidad, tr. James Darmesteter, Sacred Books of the East, Oxford: Oxford University Press, 1880.

25. Reem the Mountain with Horns

Bernhard Heller, 'Ginzberg's Legends of the Jews', *The Jewish Quarterly Review*, Vol. 24, No. 4, 1934, pp. 393–418.
Howard Schwartz, *Tree of Souls; The Mythology of Judaism*. New York: Oxford University Press, 2004.
The Bible, Psalm 22:21.

26. Tekhumiavi a Dreamscape

Samantha Hurn (ed.), *Anthropology and Cryptozoology: Exploring Encounters with Mysterious Creatures*, New York: Routledge, 2017.
Subhra Roy, 'Retracing Deep Ecology in the Reorientation of Naga Identity With Special Reference to the Select Works of Easterine Kire Iralu', *Rupkatha Journal on Interdisciplinary Studies in Humanities*, Vol. 12, No. 5, 2020, pp. 1–6.

27. Jambavan the Monkey Bear

Bhagavata Purana, IV:LVI.
Jamba Puranam.
Tulsidas, *Shri Ramacharitmanasa*, Kishkindakanda and Lankakanda.
Robert Goldman, 'Tracking the Elusive Ṛkṣa: The Tradition of Bears as Rama's Allies in Various Versions of the Rāmakathā', *Journal of the American Oriental Society*, Vol. 109, No. 4, Oct–Dec 1989, pp. 545–552.
Simon Charsley, 'Madiga and Dalit: Exploring the Heritage,' available at <www.simoncharsley.co.uk>.

28. Uchchaihshravas the Cosmic Horse

Bhagavad Gita, 10:27
Rig Veda,1:164.35.
Taittiriya Samhita, 7.1-5
Vishnu Purana, 1:12.

29. Kayutha the Cosmic Bull

Abu Yahya Zakariya' ibn Muhammad al-Qazwini, 'Ajā'ib al-makhlūqāt wa gharā'ib al-mawjūdāt' (Wonders of Creation), in Edward William Lane, *Arabian Society in the Middle Ages: Studies from the Thousand and One Nights*, 1883, available at <gutenberg.org>.
The Holy Qur'ān, Surah: 65.12.

30. Nandi the Dharma Bull

Linga Purana, Part 1.7
Matsya Purana, XCIII.

Shiva Purana, 3.6–7 and 3.23.

31. Buddha the White Elephant

Buddhist Birth-Stories (Jataka Tales), tr. T. W. Rhys Davids, 2016, available at <gutenberg.org>.
Chaddanta Jataka.
Silava Jataka.

32. Mahisa the Majestic

'Devi Mahatmaya', *Markandeya Purana*, 80.21–44.
Alf Hiltebeitel, 'The Indus Valley "Proto-Śiva", Reexamined through Reflections on the Goddess, the Buffalo, and the Symbolism of Vāhanas', *Anthropos*, Bd. 73, H. 5./6., pp. 767–797, 1978.
Kalika Purana, 62, 104–105, and 80.
Skanda Purana, 3.10–12.

33. Airavata the King of Elephants

The Elephant Lore of the Hindus (Nilkantha's Matanga-Lila), tr. F. Edgerton, Delhi: Motilal Banarasi Das, 1985.
The Mahabharata, Adi Parva.
Tulsidas, *Shri Ramacharitmanasa*, Aranyakanda.
Somadevabhatt, *Kathasaritsagara*, tr. Pandit Kedarnath Sharma Saraswat.

34. The Holy Cow: Prithvi Surabhi Dharma

Frank J. Korom, 'Holy Cow! The Apotheosis of Zebu, or Why the Cow Is Sacred in Hinduism', *Asian Folklore Studies*, 2000, Vol. 59, No. 2, pp. 181–203, 2000.

Bhagavata Purana, Vol. 2, IV.18.7.

Devi Bhagavatam, Book 9, XLIX.

Norman Brown, 'The Sanctity of the Cow in India', *The Economic Weekly*, 1964, p. 251, qtd in Frank J. Korom, 'Holy Cow! The Apotheosis of Zebu, or Why the Cow Is Sacred in Hinduism', *Asian Folklore Studies*, Vol. 59, No. 2, 2000, pp. 181–203.

The Hymns of the Rigveda, 1.32.2, tr. Ralph T. H. Griffith, Benaras: E. J. Lazarus and Co., 1890.

Vishnu Purana, 4.24.

OTHER CREATURES OF AIR, WATER, AND LAND: WORMS, INSECTS, REPTILES, AND DRAGONS

35. Azhi Dahaka the Corruptor of the Order

'Azdaha,' Encyclopædia Iranica.

Abolqasem, *Shahnameh: The Persian Book of Kings*, tr. Dick Davis, New York: Penguin Books, 2001, p. 200.

Hom Yasht 9, v. 7–8, tr. L. H. Mills, *Sacred Books of the East* (American edn), New York: Christian Literature Co., 1898.

Ram Yasht XV, Chapters V–VI, tr. James Darmesteter, *Sacred Books of the East* (American edn), New York: Christian Literature Co., 1898.

36. The Serpent in the Garden of Eden

King James Bible, Mark 1:13, Revelations 12.3–4 and 7–9, Luke 11:15–19, and Matthew 12:24–27.

John K. Bonnell, 'The Serpent with a Human Head in Art and in Mystery Play', *American Journal of Archaeology*, Vol. 21, No. 3, Jul–Sep 1917, pp. 255–91.

The Bible, Genesis 3.1-119.
The Bible, Revelations 12.3-4 and 7-9.
'The Temptation of Adam and Eve,' (painting), Mariotto Albertinelli, 1509–1513, Wikimedia Commons.

37. Shesha Naag the Endless One

Mahabharata, Adi and Vana Parvas.
Tulsidas, *Shri Ramacharitmanasa*, Kishkindakanda XL.

38. Takshaka the Ophidian Epitome

Mahabharata, Adi and Svaragarohana Parvas.

39. Pakhangpa the Guardian Python

'Anji Paphal', Indira Gandhi Rashtriya Manav Sanghralaya (IGRMS), see <igrms.gov.in/en/whatsnew/anji-paphal>.
Cheithou Yuhlung, 'The Identity of Pakhangpa: The Mystical Dragon-Python God of Chothe of Manipur', 28 August 2013.
Mutua Bahadur, 'Illustrated Manuscripts of Manipur: Part 1', E-PAO, 2 Feb 2010.

40. Mandeha the Sandhill

'Decoding: The Ramayana Connection of the Gympie Pyramid Brisbane in Australia', *The Hindu Portal*, 20 Aug 2019.
Ramayana, Kishkindakanda XL.
Rebecca Morelle, 'Ancient Migration: Genes Link Australia with India', *BBC*, 14 Jan 2013.

41. Bhramari the Beehive Goddess

Devi-Bhagavata Purana, Book 10, XIII.

42. Shamir the Stone-cutting Worm

Louis Ginzberb, *The Legends of the Jews*, Vols. 1–4, Philadelphia: The Jewish Publication Society of America, 1925.
The Bible, Exodus, 20:32.
The Holy Qur'ān, Surah: 34:14.

43. The Caterpillar Man

William Smith, 'Ao Naga Folktales', *Folklore*, Vol. 37, No. 4, 31 Dec 1926, pp. 371–394.

44. Ants—Teachers of Humility

Brahmavaivarata Purana, Krishna-Janma Khanda.
Louis Ginzberg, *The Legends of the Jews*, Vol. 4, Ch. V, 1909.

CREATIONS OF AMALGAM

45. Buraq the Shining One

The Holy Qur'ān, Surah: 17.1.
Muhammad Ibn Ishaq, *The Life of Muhammad: A Translation of Ishaq's Sirat Rasul Allah*, tr. A. Guillaume, Karachi: Oxford University Press, 1967.
Ron Buckley, 'The Burāq: Views from the East and West,' *Arabica*, T. 60, Fasc. 5, 2013, pp. 569–601.

46. Nariphon the Plant Women

Justin Thomas McDaniel, *The Lovelorn Ghost and the Magical Monk: Practicing Buddhism in Modern Thailand*, New York: Columbia University Press, 2011.

'Vessantara Jataka', *The Jataka*, Vol. 6, tr. E. B. Cowell and W. H. D. Rouse, 1907, Internet Sacred Texts Archive.

47. Adne Sadeh the Human Plants

Howard Schwartz, *Tree of Souls: The Mythology of Judaism*, New York: Oxford University Press, 2004.
Louis Ginzberg, *The Legends of the Jews*, Vol. IV, Ch. 1, 1909, Internet Sacred Texts Archive.

48. Dadhikravana the Bird–Horse and Hayagriva the Horse-headed

Bhagavata Purana
Devi Bhagavatam, Book 1.V.
The Hymns of the Ṛigveda, 4:39–40, tr. Ralph T. H. Griffith, Benaras: E. J. Lazarus and Co., 1890.
Som Raj Gupta, 'Kaṭha Upaniṣad', *The Word Speaks to the Faustian Man*, Vol. 1, Ch. 2, Sec. 2, Verse 2, p. 321.

49. Yali a Synthesis in Stone

'Vyala', *A Sanskrit English Dictionary*, ed. M. Monier Williams, Michigan: Claredon Press, 1995.
Ar. Meenal Kumar, 'Pillars [stambha]–the Supportive Elements of Hindu Temples', *International Journal of Current Research*, Vol. 10, Issue 6, 28 June 2018, pp. 70223–28.
Akhaya Kumar Mishra, 'Representation of Birds and Animals in the Temple Art of Konarak', *International Journal of English Language, Literature and Humanities*, Vol. 111, Issue 111, May 2015.
Crispin Branfoot, 'Expanding Form: The Architectural Sculpture of the South Indian Temple, ca. 1500–1700',

Artibus Asiae, 2002, Vol. 62, No. 2, 2002, pp. 189–245.
Matsya Purana Part 1, XCIII.

50. Chalkydri the Angels of the Sun

Gustav Davidson, *A Dictionary of Angels: Including the Fallen Angels*, New York: The Free Press, 1971.
Rutherford H. Platt, Jr., *The Forgotten Books of Eden*, 1926, Internet Sacred Texts Archive.

51. Kinnara—Perhaps a Man

Bhallāṭiya Jātaka (504), *The Jataka, Vol. IV*, tr. W. H. D. Rouse, 1901, Internet Sacred Texts Archive.
Canda-Kinnara Jātaka (485), ibid.
Mahabharata, Anushasana Parva.

52. Sharabha a Shiva Avatar

Shiva Purana Part 111, 12.1-47.

53. Gandabherunda a Vishnu Avatar

K. N. V. Sastri, 'The Political Theory of Mysore as a Dekhan Power (1700–1800)', *The Indian Journal of Political Science*, Vol. 3, No. 4, April–June 1942, pp. 380–83.
M. B. Emeneau, 'Studies in the Folk Tales of India: III: Jain Literature and Kota Folk-Tales', *Journal of the American Oriental Society*, Vol. 67, No. 1, Jan–Mar 1947, pp. 1–13.
S. Srikanta Shastri, 'Evolution of the Gandabherunda', <www.srikanta-sastri.org/evolution-of-the-gandabherunda>.
Vidya Dehejia and Rishard Davis, 'Addition, Erasure, and Adaptation: Interventions in the Rock-Cut Monuments of

Māmallapuram', *Archives of Asian Art*, Vol. 60, 2010, pp. 1–18.

54. Navagunjara a Unity

Sarala Das, *Odia Mahabharata*, 2nd Khanda, Madhya Parva.
Sumanyu Satpathy and Jatindra K. Nayak, 'Sarala Mahabharata: Introduction', *Indian Literature*, Vol. 58, No. 3 (281), Delhi: Sahitya Akademi, May/June 2014, pp. 7–14.

55. Harrapan Chimera

Dennys Frenez and Massimo Vidale, 'Harappan Chimaeras as "Symbolic Hypertexts". Some Thoughts on Plato, Chimaera and the Indus Civilization', *South Asian Studies*, Vol. 28, No. 2, 2012, pp. 107–30.